7 BILLION LIVES ARE IN DANGER.
13 STRANGERS WITH TERRIFYING NIGHTMARES.
1 ENEMY WILL STOP AT NOTHING TO DESTROY US ALL.

MY NAME IS SAM.
I AM ONE OF THE LAST THIRTEEN.
OUR BATTLE CONTINUES . . .

This one's for Malcolm—JP.

First American Edition 2014
Kane Miller, A Division of EDC Publishing

Illustrations by Chad Mitchell
Design by Nicole Stofberg

First published by Scholastic Australia Pty Limited in 2014
This edition published under license from Scholastic Australia Pty Limited.

Cover photography: Blueprint © istockphoto.com/Adam Korzekwa; Parkour Tic-Tac © istockphoto.com/Willie B. Thomas; Climbing wall © istockphoto.com/microgen; Leonardo da Vinci (Sepia) © istockphoto.com/pictore; Gears © istockphoto.com/-Oxford-; Mechanical blueprint © istockphoto.com/teekid; Circuit board © istockphoto.com/Bjorn Meyer; Map © istockphoto.com/alengo; Grunge drawing © istockphoto.com/aleksandar velasevic; World map © istockphoto.com/Maksim Pasko; Internet © istockphoto.com/Andrey Prokhorov; Inside clock © istockphoto.com/LdF; Space galaxy © istockphoto.com/Sergii Tsololo; Sunset © istockphoto.com/Joakim Leroy; Blue flare © istockphoto.com/YouraPechkin; Global communication © istockphoto.com/chadive samanthakamani; Earth satellites © istockphoto.com/Alexey Popov; Girl portrait © istockphoto.com/peter zelei; Student & board © istockphoto.com/zhang bo; Young man serious © istockphoto.com/Jacob Wackerhausen; Portrait man © istockphoto.com/Alina Solovyova-Vincent; Sad expression © istockphoto.com/Shelly Perry; Content man © istockphoto.com/drbimages; Pensive man © istockphoto.com/Chuck Schmidt; Black and pink © istockphoto.com/blackwaterimages; Punk Girl © istockphoto.com/Kuzma; Woman escaping © Jose antonio Sanchez reyes/Photos.com; Young running man © Tatiana Belova/Photos.com; Gears clock © Jupiterimages/Photos.com; Young woman © Anomen/Photos.com; Explosions © Leigh Prather | Dreamstime.com; Landscape blueprints © Firebrandphotography | Dreamstime.com; Jump over wall © Ammentorp | Dreamstime.com; Mountains, CAN © Akadiusz Iwanicki | Dreamstime.com; Sphinx Bucegi © Adrian Nicolae | Dreamstime.com; Big mountains © Hoptrop | Dreamstime.com; Sunset mountains © Pklimenko | Dreamstime.com; Mountains lake © Janmika | Dreamstime.com; Blue night sky © Mack2happy | Dreamstime.com; Old writing © Empire331 | Dreamstime.com; Young man © Shuen Ho Wang | Dreamstime.com; Abstract cells © Sur | Dreamstime.com; Helicopter © Evren Kalinbacak | Dreamstime.com; Aeroplane © Rgbe | Dreamstime.com; Phrenology illustration © Mcarrel | Dreamstime.com; Abstract interior © Sur | Dreamstime.com; Papyrus © Cebreros | Dreamstime.com; Blue shades © Mohamed Osama | Dreamstime.com; Blue background © Matusciac | Dreamstime.com; Sphinx and Pyramid © Dan Breckwoldt | Dreamstime.com; Blue background2 © Cammeraydave | Dreamstime.com; Abstract shapes © Lisa Mckown | Dreamstime.com; Yellow Field © Simon Greig | Dreamstime.com; Blue background3 © Sergey Skrebnev | Dreamstime.com; Blue eye © Richard Thomas | Dreamstime.com; Abstract landscape © Crazy80frog | Dreamstime.com; Rameses II © Jose I. Soto | Dreamstime.com; Helicopter © Sculpies | Dreamstime.com; Vitruvian man © Cornelius20 | Dreamstime.com; Scarab beetle © Charon | Dreamstime.com; Eye of Horus © Charon | Dreamstime.com; Handsome male portrait © DigitalHand Studio/Shutterstock.com; Teen girl © CREATISTA/Shutterstock.com; Iguacu Falls panorama© istockphoto.com/Hanis; Christ the Redeemer, Rio De Janeiro © Renato Machado | Dreamstime.com; Morning in the rain forest © istockphoto.com/FernandoAH; Ipanema Beach at nightfall © istockphoto.com/zxvisual; Man climbing waterfall in Brazil © istockphoto.com/micahgoulart; Rio de Janeiro © istockphoto.com/JohanSjolander; Sugar Loaf Mountain © istockphoto.com/Nikada; Mini Globe Brazil, Chile and Argentina © istockphoto.com/abzee; Aerial photo © istockphoto.com/JohnnyLye; Rain forest green tropical Amazon © Dirk Ercken | Dreamstime.com; Tourist boat at Iguacu Falls © istockphoto.com/gregul; Boat in the Amazônia © Antonio De Azevedo Negrão | Dreamstime.com; Treasure © tacartoons | Dreamstime.com; Way through forest © Kettaphoto | Dreamstime.com; Exit © Ollirg | Dreamstime.com; From the cave © Olga Khoroshunova | Dreamstime.com; Stairs into a cave © Kanusommer | Dreamstime.com; Small plane in blue cloudy sky © Robertsj | Dreamstime.com; El Dorado © Kerem Gogus | Dreamstime.com; El Dorado © Kerem Gogus | Dreamstime.com; Security monitor © istockphoto.com/sweetandsour; Aztec gold © istockphoto.com/Astova; Paragliding over a rolling landscape © istockphoto.com/Ogphoto; M49A1 surface trip-flare © Robert Sholl | Dreamstime.com. Internal photography: p104, White old paper © Jiri Hera | Dreamstime.com

For information contact:
Kane Miller, A Division of EDC Publishing
PO Box 470663
Tulsa, OK 74147-0663
www.kanemiller.com
www.edcpub.com
www.usbornebooksandmore.com

Library of Congress Control Number: 2013945816

Printed and bound in the United States of America
1 2 3 4 5 6 7 8 9 10
ISBN: 978-1-61067-269-6

THE LAST THIRTEEN

BOOK FIVE

JAMES PHELAN

Kane Miller
A DIVISION OF EDC PUBLISHING

PREVIOUSLY

Sam is shocked when Alex rescues him from Solaris at the Berlin Zoo, however Solaris escapes with Xavier's Gear.

After Sam has recovered, he goes with the Professor to Paris to meet with the Council of Dreamers. While in Paris, Sam finds Zara, the next of the last 13, creating an evacuation at the Louvre museum so he can meet her. He must convince Zara of their joint quest but is wary of her Enterprise Agent parents interfering.

Eva and the others work to hide Sam's identity as unwanted publicity of his adventures has brought him to the attention of the international authorities.

Alex waits anxiously to share what he knows about Stella with the Enterprise director. At the Enterprise, he learns more about how the race for the Dream Gate is disrupting the world's dreaming patterns. When he discovers that Stella is undertaking a covert mission in Austria, his concerns deepen.

At the Council meeting, the Councillors are divided. Sam is confronted by one vocal critic, Mac, who walks out, taking many of the Council with him. The Professor urges Sam not to lose focus and to pursue his dreams with Zara.

Sam and Zara find her home ransacked, and they seek help from Zara's father, who assures Sam he only wants to protect her. He fights off Hans' men as they flee to the Council, only to find signs of foul play and the remaining Councillors gone.

Forced to the top of the Eiffel Tower with both Hans and Solaris in pursuit, Sam and Zara BASE jump from the Tower and miraculously manage to escape. They drive to da Vinci's workshop in the French countryside to find the Gear Zara has dreamed of.

Stella bombs the Academy in attack helicopters, mercilessly killing and injuring students and Guardians. Eva and the others fight bravely but their friend Pi dies in the attack.

Racing to stay ahead of their enemies, Sam and Zara find the Gear but are ambushed first by Mac and then Solaris, who steals both the Gear and the Bakhu machine. Hans has paid off the local police and takes them prisoner. There is no one left to help Sam now . . .

SAM'S NIGHTMARE

Smack. I swat the mosquito from my arm. Then another and another.

The guy opposite me laughs, then says, "Welcome to Brazil, Sam."

I look around. A river. A boat.

"Um, thanks," I say, surprise in my voice.

"I'm Pablo," the man says. We shake hands.

"Don't I know you from somewhere?" I say, trying to place the older man's friendly face.

"We saw each other, recently, but did not properly meet. It was in Paris."

"Aha—I saw you at the Council!" I say, making the connection. "You're one of the Councillors."

"Yes."

I look around to get my bearings. We're on a boat—a big, old ferry, stuffed with hundreds of passengers and tons of cargo, riding low in the brown water of what must be the Amazon River. The walkway where we stand is busy with passengers hurrying and pushing up and down the boat. Vendors have set up little shops on board, selling food and drink, trading wares and playing card games with customers. It's a small floating village, chugging its way along the epic waterway.

I'm dreaming.

"Why am I meeting you here?" I ask, adjusting the straps of my backpack over my shoulders after someone bumps past. "No offense, but you're not who I was expecting."

"I am here to tell you about this," Pablo says, warily taking a plastic-covered map from his bag.

I recognize the map, and I instinctively look up at the staggered decks above us, making sure no one is eavesdropping.

"I have studied this," Pablo says, tapping the map. It is one of the maps I discovered with Gabriella inside the book box from the Vatican library. This is a photocopy or printout, but definitely shows the same familiar lines and shapes. "I'm afraid it is not much help. But . . ."

"But?"

"Perhaps with the right guide." Pablo looks from the map to me.

"And that's not you, is it?" I ask. "So who? Who do I need?"

"I think only you know the answer to that."

"But I—I don't know anyone in Brazil . . ." I reply.

Who could possibly be my guide here?

I absently look at those around me, as if the answer will present itself in one of these faces—faces that all seem to turn towards me.

Why are they all looking at me?

"They sense you're afraid. You are looking for help and searching it out among them. You are starting to . . . change things, to alter them."

I look around again—I can't see anyone who looks like they could help me, although all the faces, old and young, are still looking back at me. The more I look, the more they stare back. The sky suddenly clouds over and the wind picks up a chill.

"This . . . this doesn't feel right," I say, backing away from the rail until I feel the solid wood wall behind me. The onboard commotion has dulled—they're no longer going about their business, no one is talking.

A panic rises inside me. "Pablo—what's going on here?"

"Sam, it's OK. This is what happens when you start *steering* things. Come, follow me," Pablo says, and we make our way through the subdued crowd to the stern of the big weary boat, above the churning of the paddles in the water. It is so quiet now, we could almost be alone.

"What's going on?" I ask again. "What is this?"

Pablo looks at me carefully. "It is as you thought, Sam," he says. "You are in a dream. Your dream. And you brought me into it. You brought all of this into it—it's your *creation*, where your subconscious mind knows you need to be."

The sun is retreating to the edge of space and the river starts to churn and bubble. The water eddies around the boat like some sort of giant water monster is down there.

If this is my creation, then how do I control it? How can I stop what I know is coming?

"Sam, you need to relax . . ." Pablo says. "Don't fight it–go with it."

I try to calm myself. The world around us returns to as it was before.

But I feel a shiver of fear run through me.

Oh no . . . if I have imagined all this, what else will I conjure up?

Solaris.

"Sam, you need to stay calm and in control, or else this *will* turn into a nightm–"

There is a loud, powerful engine noise from down the river somewhere behind us and Pablo stops talking. I search the horizon and see movement, squinting to make out the details.

"It's a boat," I say, "a speedboat."

Could be anyone . . . but they're sure in a hurry to catch up with us.

"I think . . . I think it's a friend," I say. The sun reemerges and the birds start squawking again.

"Good, you are not giving in to your fear!" Pablo says over the rising noise of the approaching speedboat engine. "Remember, you can control everything that happens in here and just as easily, you can lose control. Either way, it's up to you."

Pablo pulls a small set of binoculars from his bag and brings them to his eyes.

"Ah," he says, then passes them to me.

I look—focus to find the little craft gaining in our wake. There are nine men in the speedboat—no, eight men, and a woman. The woman I know. It's Stella, the leader of the rogue Enterprise Agents.

"OK, not friends," I say, handing the binoculars back, pleased to see that all else around me is remaining calm and normal.

Maybe I can *steer this dream. Stella or not, I can't go until I've got what I've come for.*

There's a new sound coming from the direction of the jungle. A small speck has materialized into another boat, smaller, further away and slower, but also heading towards us.

Pablo suddenly looks anxious. "Sam, it's too late. This must end now."

"What?" I ask, looking away from the approaching boats.

"Wake up."

"Why? How do I do that?" I ask. "How can I make myself wake—"

There's a hollow-sounding cough and then I see a missile streaking up from the first speedboat. It shoots high into the air and then breaks apart, revealing several smaller warheads that all race down towards the ferry.

"Quick, Sam!" Pablo says. "Find us a way out of this

before it's too—"

KLAP-BOOM!

My whole world is cloaked by fire and smoke and heat, enveloping me as I am thrown onto my back by the concussive wave. Through the shimmering heat waves I see a dark figure watching on from the shore, the form as shifting and menacing as the flames that lick at my heels. I cannot see his face, but I sense that he is happy.

No!

I try to get to my feet. My breathing is ragged, panic rising from being surrounded by flames.

Not this, anything but this.

The fire eats hungrily into the wooden structure of the boat. The wall, the floorboards, the ceiling above, are all cracking and groaning in slow disintegration. We are sinking.

Where is Pablo?

I am in the water, gulping breaths between mouthfuls of smoke and raging water. A life buoy floats past, just out of reach.

I am under the waves.

I see hands reaching down for me, twisting fingers searching through the water. I resurface briefly, gasping desperately for more air. Through blurry, water-stung eyes I can see someone reaching out to help.

As my head sinks below the flaming waves for the last time, the small boat drifts further away and I stare, defeated, at letters stenciled on the life buoy as it, too, floats away. The water surrounds me, crushing me as I look up at the fire above. But below there is only—

Silence.

SAM

"Don't look down, don't look down . . ."

Sam looked down.

"Oh, *man*."

The ground was at least eight stories below.

I can't believe I'm doing this.

Come on, stay focused. Gotta find Zara, gotta get out of here. Wherever here is.

Sam clung tightly to the side of the building, his fingers fighting for purchase in a tiny crevice in the slippery stone facade. It was raining, and nothing more than the tips of his shoes and fingers were keeping him from falling from the top floor of the apartment building. He measured the distance to go and was relieved to see that he was nearly at the next window across, which at least had a decent ledge on which he could stand and rest for a moment.

"OK, Sam, you can do this. Easy does it . . ." he said as he edged along the tiny lip of stone on the outside of the building.

Sam slipped, reaching out just in time to grab on to the steel railing outside the nearest window. He held on with one hand, panting for breath, trying to stay calm and summon the strength and focus needed to haul himself up. He looked down, beyond his dangling legs. The windows were in a row, with several now directly below him. It would be easier to drop to the next window ledge, to get down the building that way, but he couldn't do that.

Not yet.

He had to keep going *across*, along the outside of this floor of the building, to get to the next window.

Hold on, Zara, I'm almost there.

The rain fell into his eyes. His arms burned from the strain.

He shifted across, slowly, hand-to-hand, so that he could be in position to swing his legs up to the ledge.

Sam focused, breathed slowly and closed his eyes. The vision of his nightmare flashed into his mind.

He jerked his eyes back open and thought about how he'd woken up to find himself locked inside an empty room. Memories of how he and Zara had been kidnapped by Hans crowded in. But he was sure his dream had given him a glimpse of who he was meant to find. But it was so unclear, clouded by flames and water—*and fear.*

He had immediately felt the urgent need to get back to the Academy so he could reenter the dream.

But what if what Hans said is true? Is the Academy really gone?

Sam forced himself to focus on the here and now, his precarious situation at the front of his mind once more.

Get off this ledge. Free Zara. Find out what's happened.

He gritted his teeth, hauled himself up and slumped with relief on the window ledge. He paused to catch his breath again.

Below there were the wet cobbles of an old city street. At da Vinci's home outside Paris, he and Zara had been bound and hooded and thrown into the back of a van, transferred by their captors last night. The trip felt like it had taken hours so there was no way to know precisely where they now were. It was very early morning, predawn, all quiet, with only a couple of lights on in distant apartment buildings. He could not make out any landmarks.

OK, let's do this . . .

Sam stood on the ledge. Through the window he could see that this room had its door open, and the light from the hall spilled through the doorway. This room was empty, too—just a single cot bed like the room they'd put him in. The building itself, inside and out, looked old and worn.

Abandoned, perhaps?

He looked across at the next window along. Zara had been locked in there—he remembered pausing, hearing her being pushed inside, then he'd counted the paces it had taken to get to his room. The hood had been removed but his hands and feet left bound.

Now, Sam contemplated the tiny ledge before him—that

teeny, tiny lip of wet stone for his fingers and toes, along which he'd counted the paces.

"OK," he whispered to himself.

He looked down again, then took some more settling breaths.

"Come on—I've jumped off the Eiffel Tower without a parachute," Sam continued. "I can do this. One foot after the other."

One toe after the other, more like.

Sam set off, shimmying along the face of the building.

A car rumbled by below. He couldn't signal to it for help, not wanting to turn his head down and risk shifting his center of balance.

Concentrate!

He needed to keep as flat as possible against the wall so that he didn't fall off the building.

Keep moving, almost there.

Sam inched along, sliding the toe of his shoe across, meeting it with the other, repeating the process, and when the window with the large windowsill was within reach—

He stepped out onto the sill. His hands and legs were shaking from the effort. Sam squinted to make out details in the dark room inside.

Please be the right room. Is she in there? Maybe she's been moved.

Sam could not make out anything in the darkness

inside so he swallowed hard, then tapped lightly against the window.

Nothing. He waited a minute, then tried again.

TAP, TAP, TAP.

"Argh!" A face suddenly appeared from the darkness and Sam instinctively leaned back in shock, losing his footing, his arms flailing to make up for the sudden shift in balance. He managed to grab on to the window frame and steady himself.

Zara looked at him, her own shocked expression breaking into a big smile around her cloth gag.

Sam pointed at the latch on the window and Zara nodded and shuffled closer. Her ankles were bound and when she reached for the latch, he could see her wrists were still tied too. The windows opened into the room like double doors, and Sam fell through the opening gratefully, tumbling onto the bare floorboards.

"Here," he said in a whisper, getting up to untie her gag and then her wrists. His own hands were shaking from the adrenaline still pumping through his body.

"How did you become free?" Zara asked in her soft French accent.

"With a lot of effort," Sam said, undoing the tightly knotted rope around her ankles. He held up his arms in the dim light to reveal dark crimson marks circling each of his wrists. Zara winced. "Actually, I used my teeth."

"You ate through the rope?" Zara said. "Incredible!"

"I'm kidding," Sam said, laughing and rubbing the red marks around his wrists. "I used a sharp bit of the broken bed frame in my room to cut myself free. So, do you know where we are?"

Zara shook her head.

"I have no clue either, but I reckon we traveled for hours. Take a look out there."

"We're still in France!" she said, putting her head out the open window.

"You're sure?" Sam asked, joining her and looking down at the streets around them.

"The cars, the road—there, that sign!" she pointed to a sign he could barely make out by the dim streetlight below.

She took a deep breath in through her nose. "We're near the sea . . . Marseilles, maybe?"

"Great, that's a start," Sam said, looking down at the long drop to the street.

"So what now?" Zara asked.

"We get out of here."

EVA

Eva looked away from the sheets covering the bodies, not wanting to see. She didn't know how many there were under there, but one was too many, and there was far more than one. A violent sob threatened to break through and overcome her.

I'm still alive.

The stones from the destroyed Academy building lay in piles. Eva looked around at the Guardians and Academy staff who remained on the Swiss mountaintop, working through the night to find anyone still trapped in the rubble, blackened with the smoke of the spot fires that broke out after the attack.

A flashlight beam danced over her. "How are you holding up?" Tobias asked, stopping beside Eva and passing her a bottle of water.

"I'm not, really," Eva said truthfully. She felt numb, as if functioning only automatically, from outside herself. She put down her shovel and had a drink. The water was cool down her throat and she drank the full bottle in a few gasping gulps.

"Eva," Tobias said. "You should rest."

"When are we going to be able to leave?" Eva said to him, ignoring his advice. She put down the empty bottle and picked up her shovel again, ready to keep clearing debris.

"We'll have to wait for dawn, for the weather to clear," Tobias said as he gently took the shovel from her hands. Eva realized she was far too tired to object.

Tobias dragged another huge, broken wooden beam onto the raging fire that burned near them. The heat staved off the cold mountain air, and every now and then the people would come over and warm themselves before setting off to sift through the ruins once more. His face was drawn and tired.

I probably look just as bad.

"More help is on its way, Eva, we're not alone."

Eva nodded, holding out her hands to heat them by the fire. There were still a few small patches of glowing embers in the remains of the old monastery, even though the attack had happened hours ago. She knew that the only road out was impassable—a direct missile hit had triggered that whole side of the mountain to avalanche, taking the road with it.

The last medical chopper had left over two hours before, taking more wounded students and injured Guardians. Gabriella had gone with them, bandaged around the head, Lora helping her on board. Xavier had wanted to stay but he was needed to assist in caring for the wounded during the flight.

"Until these strong winds drop a little, it's too dangerous for the helicopters to come back to get us. They'll be back when they can and we'll resume the search for survivors at first light," Tobias said, sitting down in a makeshift shelter under a section of collapsed roof.

"OK," Eva said, taking a seat next to him. She felt tired, as though stopping her search and rescue efforts had brought with it a new wave of exhaustion and desperation.

Maybe I could rest for just a little while. Dream of some place, far from here, somewhere happy . . .

"They won't be back," Tobias said, his tone resolute as he looked absently into the fire. "Stella, I mean. They achieved what they set out to do."

The fire crackled and sparked amid the silence between the two of them. Eva had known this was a dangerous time, but even now she could not comprehend how things had suddenly turned so deadly. It didn't seem real, seeing the shapes lying underneath the stark white sheets.

And Pi . . .

Eva struggled to suppress another sob. Most of the staff and students had been able to get out in time, helped by the Guardians who put their lives on the line to ensure that the Dreamers were evacuated safely. Many brave Guardians had not been so lucky.

"Thanks," Eva said finally, "for everything."

"You don't need to thank me."

"But you saved me, out in the snow before," she said. "And now, because of you, many of us here are alive. How did you know where to be?"

Tobias shrugged modestly. "I dreamed something terrible was coming—but I had no idea it would be this bad, not in my wildest of dreams. I had suspected deep rifts in the Academy and the Council for a while now, and we had information about rogue elements operating within the Enterprise. I didn't know exactly what I was waiting for, but I knew I had to wait. And it had to be alone."

"We were so lucky you were here," Eva said again.

"We will need even more luck now. There's still a long way to go," Tobias said. "But I truly believe that as long as Sam is leading us, we can do this."

"You think he's OK?"

"Yes," Tobias said, nodding, a small smile on his lips. "Sam's out there still, no doubt dreaming of more Dreamers to come. We are right to believe in him, of that I am certain."

SAM

"So, how do we escape Hans and his men?" Zara said. "Wait—we're not jumping again?"

Sam nearly laughed, remembering Zara's reaction to them BASE jumping from the Eiffel Tower. "I don't think jumping to the street is a safe option this time," Sam said, looking out the window at the darkness below, occasionally broken by the headlights of passing traffic. "It wasn't exactly a smooth, or accurate, landing last time, remember? And that was in broad daylight. There's not much my Stealth Suit can do for us if we drop in front of a truck."

He checked the room for anything they could use to help them escape. Like his room, this one was bare and the heavy wooden door was locked from the outside.

"We could try climbing down the outside of the building," Sam said, gathering up the two short ropes from the floor.

"That won't get us down to the ground," Zara said, looking at the rope that had been used to tie her up.

"Maybe it won't have to," Sam said, looking out the window down to the next ledge below. "Yeah, maybe . . ."

Sam tied the two ropes together to make a single longer

one. He tied one end of the rope to the iron handrail at the windowsill, then dangled it down to the window directly underneath. Too short. He glanced around the room, his eyes alighting on the broken mattress on the floor. A torn, dirty sheet lay across it. Sam pulled the sheet off and tied it on to the end of the rope, tossing it back out the window.

Yes!

"We slide down the rope to the next floor," Sam said, "then bust into that room, climb in and escape through the building, down to the ground floor."

Zara looked down at the rope and sheet dangling outside, and the long drop to the street.

"Bust in?"

Sam nodded and smiled. "Trust me."

Sam pushed hopefully against the window in front of him and was relieved when it swung open at his touch. Inside, it was dark and quiet. It was an apartment, or at least it used to be, but it was now as desolate as the rest of the building—unoccupied and deserted a long time ago . . . until Hans arrived.

So far, so good.

Sam looked up to Zara peering out from the window above and whispered, "Come on down."

He watched as she tentatively put her weight on the

rope and shimmied down towards the ledge where he waited and caught her, helping her into the room.

Sam put his finger to his lips and motioned for silence as they looked around the empty apartment, walking as quietly as they could across the creaking wooden floorboards.

It was much the same as the sparse rooms they'd been locked in, empty but for a few shadowy shapes of furniture, some draped in dusty sheets.

"OK," Sam said, relaxing a little. They crept into what must have once been a spacious living room. An old coffee table still sat in the corner, complete with a stack of unopened mail, and most importantly, a phone.

I wonder . . .

Sam tentatively lifted the handset and, incredibly, heard the soft hum of the dial tone.

"It's still connected!" he exclaimed in surprise, the unexpected stroke of luck making him inadvertently drop his guard.

"Shhhh!" Zara hissed worriedly. They both froze on the spot, listening for footsteps outside in the hallway. It was quiet.

"I'll call the Academy," Sam whispered.

"Are you sure?" Zara said, still sounding anxious. "Shouldn't we get out of here first? What if they notice we're missing?"

Sam thought for a moment. "My friends will be able

to help us. We might not get the chance to call again," he said.

"OK," Zara agreed, "but be quick." She continued to listen for noises beyond the front door, her face tense.

Sam dialed Lora's phone number and she answered on the third ring.

"Lora, it's Sam—"

"Sam! Where are you?"

"I'm not sure," he replied, quickly running through what had happened since he'd seen her last—da Vinci's workshop, trying to escape, Mac turning traitor and Solaris taking the Gear and the Bakhu machine. Finally he told her about Hans and the German Guardians kidnapping them.

"You've been through so much," Lora said. "I know how devastated you must be that Solaris took the Gear. But you can't imagine how relieved I am to hear from you."

"Yeah," Sam replied. "This time the Gear was in, or rather was part of, a box. And Zara's Gear was some kind of, I don't know, like a toothed axle—like it might form the middle part of the machine that all the other Gears work on or around."

"I'm just glad you're OK. You need to get out of there, but you'll have to leave the line open, so we can trace the call and find you. It may take some time." Lora hesitated, then continued, "Our equipment is down so I'm relying on a contact in the Swiss police until Jedi gets things up and running again. Can you get to someplace safe nearby to hide and call me back? As soon as we have a fix on your position, we'll head there."

"OK," he said. "But hang on, why is the Academy equipment not working?" Hans' words echoed in Sam's head, "the Academy is no more . . . blown into dust . . ."

Surely it couldn't be true? Could it?

There was a brief pause before Lora said anything and Zara could see the concern building on Sam's face.

"The Academy's main campus was attacked," Lora said finally.

No!

Sam listened silently, shock etched on his face as Lora explained how Stella had led her team of Agents to the Swiss campus and destroyed it.

"And Eva's still up there?" Sam said finally.

"She is, but we'll pick her up at first light as soon as the weather clears," Lora said. "Don't worry, Tobias is there with her."

"*What!*" Sam nearly dropped the phone in surprise.

"He's alive, Sam. He helped us. Without him, we would have had many more casualties."

Where's he been all this time—and why didn't he let me know he was OK?

Sam turned to look at Zara, sensing the fear and impatience to leave, to escape this place.

"Look, Lora, there's something else. I think I've had my

next dream, but I'll have to tell you later, we need to get away from here."

"Agreed. I've just arrived in London so I'll coordinate our efforts from here. Stay safe."

"We will."

Sam turned to Zara. "They're coming to get us, let's go."

They went to the front door of the apartment and listened intently.

"What if those guys are out there?" Zara whispered.

"Don't worry," Sam replied with a hushed voice. But he'd heard guards outside his room all night—talking and pacing. Sam hoped that there'd be no reason for Hans or his men to be on another floor.

Time to find out.

"We'll have to chance it," Sam whispered. "Besides, it seems like Hans is only using the floor above. This place looks like it's been empty for a while, right?"

There was a quiet thud outside their door and Zara jumped in fright.

Sam again held his finger to his lips. Zara nodded and they stood there, silent, listening with their ears against the wooden door. When all was quiet again, Sam took a breath, turned the lock and opened the door a couple of inches.

After peering out carefully into the corridor, they slipped out, the telephone receiver swinging on its cord in the room behind them.

ALEX

Alex headed for the makeshift operations center across the street from the still smoldering Enterprise skyscraper. With the Enterprise headquarters now cordoned off while firefighters and the police tried to make the structure safe, the uninjured Enterprise staff were gathering at the emergency meeting point in a building opposite.

A handful of Agents had been taken to the hospital by ambulance, but thanks to the Enterprise's efficient evacuation procedures, no one had been too seriously hurt.

Inside the building, the corridor was abuzz with Agents and support staff, rushing here and there with equipment, desperately trying to repair the damage and salvage what they could. They were also trying to make sense of what just happened. He caught snippets of conversation as he walked by, much of it he already knew.

"Stella went rogue!"

"Matrix destroyed the computer lab . . ."

"We're out of the race now!"

"I heard there's another hidden site."

Phoebe came down the hallway towards him. "Alex,

are you sure you're OK?" she asked, pointing to a graze on Alex's cheek.

"Really, Mom, I'm fine." Alex brushed her concern away. "I'm just looking for someone; I'll be right back."

Alex kept moving until he came to a temporary medical bay, spotting the person he was searching for.

Shiva was sitting up in a bed, typing away on a laptop. He looked a lot better than when Alex had last seen him—he had a bandage wrapped around his head and a bruised and swollen eye, but there was fire in those eyes.

"Hey," Shiva said, smiling.

"Hey, yourself," Alex replied, pulling the curtain closed behind him. "How are you feeling?"

Shiva flicked back the covers—he was fully dressed, shoes and all.

"Ha!" Alex laughed. "You keen to get back to work because of your new promotion?" Following the devastating act of betrayal when Matrix joined Stella's rogue element, Shiva had been immediately promoted to his position as the head of the IT department—news that pleased Alex.

The curtain was pulled back and the director stepped into the cubicle space. "I thought I'd find you two together," he said. "You OK, Shiva?"

"Back on deck, sir, ready as ever," Shiva replied. "I know I'm needed."

"Indeed. And we'll all have double duty to do, now we've lost so many to the other side," Jack sighed. "But we're not alone in this. As you might know, the Enterprise and the Academy were created by the Professor and myself a long time ago. And while we may have had a strong difference of opinion about the role of Dreamers in the world that forced us in different directions, we were never sworn enemies. We just had different ideas about the prophecy and the last 13."

"And now?" Alex asked.

"Stella's violent actions, going rogue and attacking *both* sides, has forced things to change. There is no more time for division. We must work together now. I've sent a team to the Academy to help with their search and rescue efforts in Switzerland. And teams of Agents and Guardians are already lining up to hunt down both Stella and Matrix."

"Well, I'm good to go," Alex said, motioning to Shiva. "You?"

"Buddy, I'm ready when you are," Shiva said, getting out of bed and pulling a backpack from underneath.

"Very good," Jack said. "I'll see you both soon." With that, he turned and left, Agents immediately scurrying up to him, phones in hands, questions at the ready.

It's really battle stations now . . .

"I still can't believe that Stella turned on us all like that," Shiva muttered. "Matrix, yeah, didn't surprise me that much—that guy always had a screw loose, and everyone could see it but they excused it because he was so brilliant at what he did. But there was always something not quite right about him."

"I just wish I could have raised the alarm earlier," Alex said, "when I hacked into Stella's files and realized what she was up to. That might even have prevented the attack on the Academy."

"No, I don't think so," Shiva said, shaking his head. "I mean, Stella's taken nearly half the Agents with her, there'd have been no stopping what they were going to do to your friends."

"Yep." Alex wondered again about Sam and Eva, and where they were and what they'd gone through. "I just can't believe she and Matrix and all of them did this and got away with it. I guess you . . . guess you never know, do you?"

"Know what?"

"What a traitor looks like."

Shiva nodded, lost in the thought. "Come on," he said, smiling and donning his backpack. "Let's get the next flight out of here. I hear there's not much room at Site B, so it'll be 'first in, best dressed' when it comes to accommodation and work spaces."

"So we're off to Amsterdam?" Alex said, slinging his own pack over his shoulder.

"Yep," Shiva replied as they walked.

"Good. It's closer to the Academy, and I want to see how they're getting on."

SAM

The corridor was empty, except for the small but recognizable silhouette of a cat walking slowly down the hallway. At Sam's feet were a bundle of old newspapers which, by the look of the settling dust, had just been knocked over.

Phew.

"Just a stray cat," Sam said. "Quick, there's no guards out here, let's move."

They raced down the corridor to a set of wooden doors at the end. There was an elevator in the lobby beyond, the old type with a slide-across metal safety screen. The motor was whirring noisily—someone was coming down.

"The stairs!" Sam whispered, and they tiptoed down the stairs, backs to the wall, warily checking around blind corners below as they descended to the shabby, unlit lobby. It was empty, but Sam could make out two security cameras at the exit—one watching out, the other watching in. The cameras looked old and neglected like the rest of the building, but he could see a tiny green light flickering near the lens.

I knew it couldn't be this easy!

"What are you waiting for?" Zara said quietly behind Sam, her hand on his shoulder to try to peer around.

"It's nothing," Sam replied. "Let's make for the doors and bolt."

"Bolt?"

"Run. Once we're out of here, we run, fast, and don't stop until we're a long way from here, someplace safe. Ready?"

Zara nodded.

Sam set off, racing across the tiled lobby and pulling hard on the handle of the big glass door—

Locked.

He rattled it, to no use.

Smash the glass?

Sam knocked on it—it was *very* thick glass.

A buzzer sounded.

Click.

The door opened. Zara smiled at Sam, her finger still pressing the release button on the wall. They fled out into the cool of the early morning.

They ran along the wet street, skirting around a team of street cleaners. The rising sun was starting to fill the sky with a soft glow, but Sam didn't know the time because his phone, watch, everything but his clothes, had been taken by Hans' guys. He felt glad to still be wearing the Stealth Suit at least.

"I'm not sure we *are* in France," Zara said as they ran.

"Get back!" Sam said, pulling her backward as a garbage truck flashed by through an intersection.

"Thanks," Zara said, pausing to look around more closely at a street sign.

"Wait."

"What is it?" Sam said, slowing and panting for breath. "Zara, come on."

She nodded and resumed running.

"What was it?" Sam asked her.

"We are definitely not in France anymore," Zara said, running in step next to him. "We're in Monaco."

"Stop there!"

Sam turned as he heard the shout. Behind the group of street cleaners were four of Hans' German Guardians, running towards them. One of the bigger guys knocked over a cleaner, who shouted obscenities and waved his fist.

"Faster, *come on!*" Sam said, taking Zara's hand and pulling her along with him.

They turned left at the next corner, entering an empty shopping strip and running along the road.

"Sam!" Zara said. "Turn right!"

He saw it too—a tiny walkway between the buildings and they zipped into it. It was barely wide enough for the two of them to fit side by side but no sooner had they entered it than the tiny cobbled path gave way onto another street.

"There!" Zara said, pointing to the warmly illuminated boutique hotel across the road, dwarfed by apartment and office buildings on either side.

They ran in, Sam hurriedly shutting the doors behind them.

Zara began talking animatedly in French to a sweet-faced old lady behind the counter. The lady looked from Zara to Sam, then waved them through the staff door behind the reception area. She followed them into a small office and busied herself putting on a kettle and making three cups of tea.

"What on earth did you tell her?" Sam whispered to Zara, smiling in what he hoped was a winning way.

"That you're my brother and that we are here with our family on vacation," Zara whispered back. "I said we were walking in the city last night and we saw something we shouldn't have on one of the yachts and some dubious men have been chasing us ever since."

"She *believed* that?"

"Crazy things happen all the time in this city. People on those mega yachts get up to all kinds of mischief."

"Pour vous," the lady said to Sam, passing him a cup of tea.

"For you," Zara translated.

"Thanks," Sam said. "Merci."

The front doors to the hotel opened, the small bell above the door ringing loudly.

The woman's expression changed and she stood straighter, suddenly not so friendly, and slowly walked back out to the reception desk, closing the door gently behind her.

Through the closed door, Sam could hear her arguing in French with the man questioning her—which he could see on a little closed-circuit TV was one of Hans' Guardians. He saw her lift the telephone receiver, waving it slightly at the Guardian, before he abruptly turned and left.

Zara translated for Sam. "She told him that she hasn't seen anyone this morning. She says the police are her very good friends and that they will be here within one minute."

The lady came back into the office, once more grandmotherly and smiling. She sipped at her tea.

"Thank you," Sam said. "Merci beaucoup."

The lady replied, speaking so quickly in French that Sam couldn't even make out one familiar word.

"She would like to know if we want to use the phone to call our parents," Zara explained.

"Sure," said Sam. "Oui, merci."

The lady nodded, passing Sam a cordless handset. Sam was about to dial Lora's number, but noticed that the lady was staring at them both quizzically, as if searching their faces for something. She began speaking quickly again.

"Funny," Zara translated as the lady spoke, "she says when she slept last night, she had the strangest dream that two teenagers would come to her for help and that she would care for them until all was safe."

Sam grinned, waiting for the call to connect. "I'm not sure that is so strange."

07

EVA

Eva and Tobias didn't have to wait too long to get off the mountain. Shortly after sunrise, the weather cleared to a sunny day with a brilliant-blue sky, and with that came help in the form of the Swiss Mountain Rescue. They, and the two dozen or so people still on the mountain, were transferred via helicopters to the main terminal of Geneva airport, where they bought onward tickets to London.

It had seemed easier, perhaps safer, after the events of the last twenty-four hours, to fly on a commercial flight than to have an Academy jet pick them up.

Hide in plain sight.

She watched the faces streaming by, all of them oblivious to what had happened so close-by.

Keep walking, nothing to see here.

Tobias ordered coffee and breakfast while they waited for their boarding announcement.

"Tobias . . ." Eva said.

"Yes, Eva?" he said, glancing around the airport cafe.

"I've been wondering, why does Sam have the dreams he does?"

"You mean, why do his dreams lead him to the other Dreamers?"

Eva nodded.

Tobias added sugar to his black coffee. He took a sip, then leaned back, scratching his chin. "The truth is I don't know, and I don't think anyone really does. His ability is quite astonishing—we've not seen this kind of thing in our time. But I have some ideas as to why."

"Such as?"

"Well, he was the last of the Enterprise's Dreamer program, and that may mean he's the last of the last 13, if you like. These 13 dreams may be happening in some kind of specific order that only Sam can determine. Or, perhaps, as the very last of the Enterprise's engineered Dreamers, Sam could have been given that little bit of something *extra*."

"Extra?"

"Maybe the genetics team took his enhanced DNA dreaming genes to another level," Tobias said, "as one final gesture."

"One final *test*, you mean."

Tobias nodded and said, "Or, it could all defy explanation completely and just be who Sam is—his destiny is to be the only one who can bring all the 13 together."

"This is so confusing . . ." Eva said, pushing her breakfast away untouched. "I mean—why did the Enterprise pick me up if I'm not even one of the 13? I've not dreamed of

Solaris, or of finding a Gear from the Bakhu machine. Sam has never dreamed of me either. Actually, I haven't had a decent dream since that first one where I was aboard the helicopter and met Sam and Alex."

"Didn't Lora mention that you dreamed about my campfire across the Alps?" Tobias inquired.

"Oh, yeah . . ." Eva said absentmindedly. "I did dream that."

"It doesn't matter if you are or if you aren't one of the last 13, Eva," Tobias said, his tone reassuring. "You clearly have a lot to contribute. But if I were a betting man, I'd put my house on you being one of them."

"Really? Why?"

"Well, the Enterprise *did* pick you up. Alex, you *and* Sam. And, as the last of the engineered Dreamers, the Enterprise kept a very close eye on the three of you—that suggests they thought there was more than a good chance you would be in the last 13. Not all of the engineered Dreamers from the program's previous years appear to have been monitored so closely. And it definitely proved true in Sam's case."

"And after Sam the program was shut down?"

"Yes."

"So," Eva said, "how many Dreamers did the Enterprise make—how many people are walking around with engineered DNA or whatever?"

"That we do know," Tobias said, then took a bite of his

bacon and egg sandwich. "Ninety-nine."

"That's specific."

"They had approval for a hundred, in the current phase of testing, which spanned the last two decades or so," Tobias said, checking his watch. "Way before that, in the 1950s and 60s, when the Enterprise was a military operation, they had a couple of experimental programs. The first was an utter failure—the Dreamers they produced had nothing but terrible nightmares. The second gen, born in the late 1960s and early 1970s, fared better, but I don't think any will be part of the last 13."

"You sure know a lot about this," Eva said, looking at Tobias carefully.

"I should," Tobias said, standing up as their flight was called. "I'm one of those second-gen Dreamers."

SAM

"Welcome home, sort of," Lora said.

Sam looked out of the window and saw that their helicopter had circled around into a landing approach in the middle of an impeccably manicured playing field. It was one of many sports fields, soccer fields and running tracks spread out below them. Sam could see a rugby team going through their paces at training and another group of students on a black-watered river racing one another in sleek rowboats.

"It's huge," Zara said. "Sam, isn't it amazing?"

"Yeah, sure," Sam said. He couldn't help thinking of his school back home, when only a few weeks ago he'd been plucked out of class after he'd watched three helicopters land on *their* sports field. This school was far different. There were no less than twenty stone buildings set across sprawling grounds, the largest ones with medieval-like towers. One even had large gothic spires pointing jaggedly into the sky. "Lora, where are we?"

"Our London campus," Lora said. "We have a building here, on the grounds of a regular boarding school. Usually just around thirty students. We're moving all classes here for the rest of the Dreamer students. The Guardians are here too—it's safest for us to stick together now."

"That is a *regular* school?" Zara said. During the flight from Monaco, Sam had explained to her the functions of the Academy, how they taught new Dreamers ways to apply their special abilities—to steer and control dreams, to deal with nightmares and to reach their true potential. But she was clearly still unprepared for the reality.

"Yes," Lora replied. "It's called Knowinghouse. It's one of the great historic schools of England."

"I've heard of it," Sam said, nose pressed to the glass. "But—but don't the Academy students want to go back to their homes and families? Aren't their parents insisting on them leaving the Academy after what happened in Switzerland, to get them as far away as possible from me and the others of the last 13?"

"Yes and no," Lora said as the helicopter hovered to a touchdown on the lush green grass. "A few have gone. But most students, and their families, recognize that what is happening now is what we've all been working for, striving towards, for many, many generations. As dangerous as things may get, this is the race to the Dream Gate that every Dreamer, myself included, learned about in their first year of school and has thought about since. For so many, this is *the* adventure of a lifetime, no matter how dangerous."

"Fair enough, I suppose," Sam said, not convinced.

He thought of the cost that came with this so-called adventure, none more obvious than the price that Pi and the others had paid.

Stella better watch out the next time we meet . . .

"So," Zara said unbuckling her seatbelt, "the Academy students will study beside the normal students here?"

"That's right," Lora said, waiting for the rotors to slow and for the all clear to disembark to be called out by the pilots. "They will go to class with the regular boarders and we'll add on extracurricular Dreamer studies outside of the school hours."

"What kinds of 'extracurricular studies'?" Zara asked.

Lora smiled. "Oh, some of them you have to see to believe."

The building that the Academy used on the Knowinghouse school campus looked like a wing of an enormous medieval castle. Inside, as Sam and Zara walked quickly behind Lora, it was no less intimidating, with its vast stone halls, cold and dark. Their rapid footfalls were amplified in the cavernous space as they came to the dining hall.

There, students Sam had known from the Swiss campus greeted them, crowding around to meet Zara and to ask about what had happened in Paris. Others told him tearful stories about the terrible attack in the Alps.

"Sam!" Eva came running over and grabbed Sam in a bear hug that nearly knocked him off his feet. "Oh, I missed you . . ."

"Thanks," Sam managed to say as she squeezed him tight. "I missed you too." He stepped back to look into her eyes. "Are we—are we good? You know I didn't mean . . ."

"It's forgotten," Eva interrupted him. "So much has happened since then, I'm just so happy to see you in one piece." Her eyes started to mist over, then she forced her chin up and turned to Zara.

"This is Zara," Sam said, introducing them.

Zara leaned in and kissed Eva lightly on both cheeks, exclaiming, "I am so pleased to meet you, Eva. Sam has told me about you."

The girls smiled shyly at each other. Then Eva turned to introduce Zara to the last 13 Dreamers. "This is Gabriella. You might know her from her previous, non-Dreamer life as a celebrity singer from Italy." She almost managed to keep the edge out of her voice. Sam nudged her.

Gabriella beamed her superstar smile in greeting.

"And this is Xavier," Eva continued, "who was the last person before you to turn up in one of Sam's last 13 dreams."

Xavier turned red when Zara kissed his cheeks in greeting. Sam lightly punched Xavier on the shoulder, pleased to see his old classmate again.

"So, that makes four of us now," Xavier said. "Nine to go."

"I just need to figure out who's next," Sam said, turning to Lora. "I think it's time to talk about my dream of Brazil."

Sam glanced around the wood paneled office in the south tower of the Academy's new residence. Out the window he could see a lush cricket field and a thickly-wooded forest beyond. Everything here was so different, yet felt oddly the same. Lora, Zara and Eva sat together, discussing why it was so important for Zara to stay there with the others. Zara was relieved to hear that her parents were both safe and well.

Sam paced the room, eager to get started, to work out a way to find the next Dreamer.

If that was *my dream about the next Dreamer.*

The room had several desks, some of which were threatening to fall over from the amount of old books stacked on them. Sam turned when the door opened—a tall man in a neat three-piece suit entered, saw Sam, and smiled.

"Professor!" Sam said. Then, seeing who entered next, he nearly exploded with excitement. "Tobias!"

"Ha!" Tobias said, nearly bowled over by Sam's embrace. "Easy there, young man."

"OK," Sam said, pleased to finally see his old teacher once more.

"You've heard all about the attack, I imagine," the Professor said, sitting in the well-worn leather chair behind the desk.

"Yes," Sam replied soberly. "Lora told me on the way here."

"And how things have changed with the Enterprise since their own misfortune," he added.

"Yes, Lora told me about that too," Sam said, referring to the attack at the Enterprise's headquarters in Silicon Valley. "That was Stella as well, right?"

"Yes, she's been quite busy, along with her tech ally, Matrix," the Professor said, struggling to turn on his laptop. "Hmm, I'm lost without my secretary. I insisted Mary take some leave after the attack in Switzerland—what's wrong with this thing?"

Lora stood fuming in the middle of the room, her anger at the attack still evident in her eyes.

"There will be the opportunity to deal with Stella, I'm sure," the Professor said calmly, as if anticipating Lora's thoughts. He was pressing the power button again, trying in vain to bring the screen to life.

"At least now everyone sees her for who she really is," Sam said. "A murderous traitor."

"Yes, although it is such an extreme way to find out," Tobias said sadly. "And it would seem those at the

Enterprise have been shocked into a more rational course of action."

"But how can we really trust an alliance with the Enterprise?" Sam asked skeptically.

"Well," the Professor said, rummaging in a drawer for a power cord. "Thankfully, their assistance in notifying the authorities saved many lives. And the Enterprise have been wounded by Stella's actions just as much as we have. We are united by a common enemy—we have no choice but to trust them, and they us."

"And where's Stella and her band of traitors now?" Sam asked.

"That's a very good question," the Professor said. "And that search is something Lora will be directing."

"I've put a team together," Lora said. "We're working with the Enterprise, who are now desperate to bring her to justice."

"Hmph," the Professor said, pressing the power button again. The computer made a loud whirring sound. "Between . . . those . . . attacks . . ." he banged on the laptop and the screen went blank.

"Here," Lora said, going around to his side of the desk and tapping away at his computer. "Violence and technology aren't a good combination."

"Right, thank you," the Professor said. "Three PhDs and I can't turn on a computer. Where was I? Yes, between those two attacks, and the attack on the Council of

Dreamers, I'm afraid we are up against threats that we never imagined . . ."

He trailed off.

"Lora?" he pointed at his computer screen.

Lora moved closer, and Tobias, Sam and Zara followed, all hovering around the Professor's desk looking at a strange graphic that had taken over the computer screen.

"Could it be . . ?"

"Matrix?" Tobias finished Lora's thought.

The face on the screen suddenly turned sinister as it said, "BYE, BYE!" followed by high-pitched cackling laughter.

In a sudden instinctive movement, Lora picked up the laptop and threw it out the open window behind them.

"Everybody get down!" she yelled, diving for the floor.

KLAP-BOOM!

10

ALEX

The taxi from the airport stopped in front of an old four-story building in a row of adjoining apartments and offices that were all designed in the same, older style. On the other side of the street was a wide canal, busy with commuter and tourist boats.

Alex had not traveled outside the US until his trip to the Academy's Swiss campus, and he marveled at the new sights and sounds around him now.

"*That's* our new HQ?" Alex said.

"Yep," Shiva said. "The Enterprise managed to keep this secret by keeping it out in the open. Clever, eh?"

As Alex got their bags out and Shiva paid the driver, Phoebe emerged from the building—

"Hey, Mom." Alex ran over to Phoebe and she gave him a hug.

"Come on in," his mother said, motioning to the open front door of the building. "We'll get you set up."

"What's this next door?" Alex asked, pointing to a building that wouldn't look out of place as the house of a president or king.

"The Allard Pierson Museum. It's an archaeological museum, part of the University of Amsterdam," Phoebe explained. "I'll take you both for a tour in there when things quiet down—some of the collection has ties to Dreamers."

"Absolutely," Shiva said.

"Well, this is our new base for a while," Phoebe said, as they entered the foyer, walking by two Agents standing guard in their gray suits and white shirts. "It used to be a bank, now it's our home away from home."

"Wow . . ." Alex let out a wondrous sigh. Inside the building, the floors were set back from the main facade, so that each was a mezzanine with a balcony looking down to the entrance. The foyer was open to the ceiling under the main roof several stories above. Agents were milling around, setting up tech gear to accommodate the rapidly expanding operations in their new hub.

"We've got teams trying to track Stella and the rogue Agents," Phoebe explained as they walked across the foyer, "along with those working on capturing Solaris and the others."

"Others?" Alex asked.

"Hans and Mac," Phoebe replied.

"Mac?" Alex said.

"He was a member of the Dreamer Council and is based in the US Defense Department—so he's a formidable competitor."

"I'll get my team hacking his system, see what he

knows," Shiva said. "And see if we can't slow him down."

"Nice," Alex said. "Any word on Sam?"

"I've heard he's fine," Phoebe said as they walked deeper into the building, "and that the Academy has also relocated. They're at their London campus."

"Are they still tracking Stella's movements?" Alex asked.

"I'm afraid not," Phoebe replied. "As far as we can work out, she escaped in an attack helicopter to Austria and then made her escape via an unmarked aircraft on a flight path headed east."

"East?" Shiva said. "That's a pretty vague heading."

"Wait," Alex said, "are you saying we've *lost* her?"

Phoebe stopped by an elevator. They got in and she pressed the top button.

"I'm afraid so. Stella dropped off the radar as soon as she entered Russian airspace."

"*Russia*?" Alex said. "What's in Russia?"

"Russians," Shiva joked.

The elevator doors pinged and they stepped out. The floor was already set up with several tables and an open plan meeting office. Down at the far end, the director was with several senior Agents, talking animatedly in serious tones, probably about Stella, Alex figured, judging by how disheveled and concerned they all looked.

After what she's just done, they're worried about what she might do next . . .

11

SAM

The Professor's laptop computer exploded midair, sending pieces of plastic and metal outward in a rapidly expanding fireball that shattered the windows with an earsplitting crash.

For what felt like a long minute, no one moved or spoke. The shock swirled around the room.

"Is everybody OK?" Lora finally asked, getting to her feet.

Sam stood up slowly, turning to the others, who all seemed to be unhurt. Then he looked across at the smashed windowpanes. On the manicured grass below, the Professor's laptop was little more than tiny pieces of plastic and metal shards and silicon chips, the charred remains scorched into the lawn.

Lucky there were no students out there.

"That was a message from Matrix," Tobias said, as two Guardians stormed into the room with dart guns drawn. "He must have planted an explosive in your computer and activated it remotely."

"I believe that was meant to do more than just give me a message, Tobias," the Professor said, still in shock himself.

"And I took that laptop with me on my trip to meet with the Council in Paris, so it could have been planted by anyone there. Stella has many more people than just Matrix working with her. The Egyptian Guardians have shown a liking for blowing things up too."

Sam remembered back to that evening in New York, watching the Egyptian Guardians storming into the Museum of Natural History to blow up the Dream Stele.

"Even I have underestimated just how cautious we all need to be—at all times," the Professor sighed.

"We must search the entire campus in case there are any more explosives," Lora said, motioning over the two Guardians. She murmured urgent instructions to them. One quickly began relaying information via his handset while the other began sweeping the room with some kind of electronic device.

"They're scanning to see if there are any radio or remote waves," Lora explained. "And a full-scale search of the grounds is now underway."

"Do you think there could be more bombs?" Eva asked. She was sitting down, pale, watching the Guardian check the room.

"I could be wrong, but I don't think so," Lora said. "That was very close. Compared to what happened at the Academy this attack seemed quite specifically directed at the Professor. Nevertheless I agree we all must take extra precautions."

The Guardians declared the room all clear and left to join the sweep of the grounds.

"Yes, indeed, I believe that was meant for me," the Professor said, looking out the window, sadness in his eyes. "Perhaps it was a backup plan, after the Switzerland attack. In all my time . . . I never thought that it would come to this."

"Solaris, Stella, Hans and now Mac—they don't play by the same rules as us," Tobias said.

Sam was lost in his thoughts for a moment, running everything over again in his head. "It could have been planted even further back than Paris," he suggested, "just waiting for the day when it was needed."

The Professor nodded.

Sam looked to Eva and saw that she was really spooked. He walked over to her and gave her a reassuring hug.

"Well," the Professor said, "we can't let them scare us into submission, we must push onward. Time is clearly very much of the essence. Sam, I heard you'd had your next dream?"

"I've seen the place, but I'm not sure exactly where it is—or who the next Dreamer is," Sam said, before adding, "it's in Brazil, that much I know. I met Pablo, the Councillor, there."

"Maybe the person who tried to help you out of the water was the next Dreamer?" Eva said.

"Maybe," Sam said. Lora and the Professor exchanged

a knowing look as Sam recounted the rest of his dream, from being with Pablo on the ferry, to struggling in the torrents of the Amazon amid the fiery wreck of the boat. He explained how he saw Solaris watching, satisfied, from the shore. And the reaching hands of the blurry figure that tried to save him.

"I see . . . Sam, I think you should leave on the next flight to Brazil," the Professor said. Lora was already on her phone making travel arrangements.

"Even though I couldn't see who the Dreamer was?"

The Professor nodded and said, "I have every faith that you will."

"Tobias," the Professor said, "please notify our colleagues at the Enterprise about our plans. We don't want any further surprises or misunderstandings today."

Sam shook his head a little. It still didn't feel right to be talking about working *with* the Enterprise, and giving them information. Sam could tell the others in the room felt the same way about the uneasy but necessary alliance that had been forced upon both sides.

"At least having them onside should even up the playing field a little," Tobias said grimly.

Maybe this really is our only way to win the race.

"Jack has moved what's left of the Enterprise operations to a new site in Amsterdam," Lora said, hanging up the phone. "I'll liaise with them and organize how to move forward together."

"I'll go with Sam to Brazil," Tobias announced. "We'll meet up with Pablo, and try to find this next Dreamer."

"I'll let Pablo know you're on your way," the Professor said. "Jedi will set up the dream-reading computer package here as soon as he is able. He's down at the boathouse setting up his new computer lab."

"Boathouse?" Sam asked.

"The rowing shed, down by the river," Lora explained, "just at the edge of the forest out there. Jedi has a lab set up there. He's working to restore the backup of all the Swiss Academy's data."

"Sam, until the whole system is back online," the Professor said, "we will have to rely on all that you can remember from your dream."

"Well," Sam said, "I have remembered something else. The name of the ferry I was on, a bit of it, anyway. I remember seeing part of a word—*Roos*—printed on a life buoy."

"Good work, Sam," the Professor said. "We will start looking into that here."

"I've got you, Tobias and Xavier on the first flight to Brazil in the morning," Lora said to Sam, after typing away furiously on her phone.

"Xavier?" Sam asked, puzzled.

He looked to the Professor who simply smiled and said, "Yes, it would seem he may have a part to play."

"We received a call from Pablo yesterday to say a

package had arrived at his university," Lora added. "It's addressed to Xavier Dark, Junior."

"We must trust in these coincidences that are not coincidences at all," the Professor said.

Sam nodded and said, "I understand. You can count on us."

"We'll have Pablo meet us at the airport with all the Brazilian Guardians," Tobias said, standing. "Sam—let's find Xavier, and get packed and ready."

"Wait, there's something else," Sam said, standing and pausing by the door. "My backpack—it's back in Monaco, with Hans."

"What was in there?" Lora asked.

"My phone. And on it, a copy of the maps that I found hidden in the Vatican library."

"So now Hans has a copy . . ." Lora said, the revelation sitting heavy with her.

"He would have found a way to get there anyway," the Professor said. "We just have to move faster. Are you sure you feel up to it, Sam?"

"Going out into the field?" Sam said. "Absolutely."

"Good," the Professor said. "We'll see about steering your dreams back to the point where you woke up and see if you can see that next Dreamer."

"I can help with that," Tobias said.

"Excellent." The Professor stood and looked at the damaged windows from the explosion. "Let's meet again tonight, yes? Oh, and Sam, pop down to see Jedi if you have a moment before you leave. I think he has something for you."

12

"Wow!" Sam said, looking around at the unexpected sight.

The boathouse of the Academy's London campus looked ordinary on the outside, a squat wooden structure by the river filled with old boats covered in a good layer of dust and cobwebs. It was what he found down the steep stone stairs, after following the tracks in the dust, which astonished him.

The old wooden shed was merely a shell for a very hi-tech basement. Several leather lounge chairs were grouped around a glass-topped coffee table, while music pumped through from the shiny stereo perched on the shelf on the far wall. The rest of the space was taken over by computer tables already covered in screens and equipment, some set up, some in the process of being unpacked from large steel cases.

"Yo, Sam!" Jedi exclaimed at once. He was shorter than Sam, twenty-something, with a patchy beard and scruffy hair to match. "Good to see you, my man."

"Hey, Jedi, you too," Sam said, gazing around the room.

There were hundreds of boxes of game consoles being unpacked and sorted by a class of senior students. "Looks like you've got your work cut out for you."

"Yep," Jedi replied, pointing and directing where the consoles were to be lined up and connected. "I heard you got into a bit of a jam on that last trip."

"Yeah, a few times," Sam said. "Still, nothing like what you had goin' on."

"Too true," Jedi sighed. "But tell me, how was the jump from the Eiffel Tower?" His eyes went wide with anticipation.

"Pretty horrifying," Sam began, his voice deadpan before breaking into a grin and adding, "but then totally awesome!"

"I knew it!" Jedi clapped Sam on the back. "Good work, man. Now . . ." He plugged in more power boards and sparks leapt out, the lights overhead flickering. He looked at Sam and followed his gaze. The setup here seemed far less sophisticated than Jedi's lab in the Swiss mountains.

"I miss Old Betsy," Jedi said, sitting down to lean back in his chair. "She was my first. Supercomputer that is. Can't believe she's gone . . ." Jedi trailed off and Sam didn't quite know what to say.

If this is where Jedi and the Academy are going to take the digital fight to Matrix, then we might be in trouble.

"Well," Jedi said, "as soon as I get this system up and running, I am going to war. I'll start with some denial-of-service attacks. Get Matrix offline and try my hardest to *keep* him offline."

"Nice," Sam said, watching students unpack console after console.

"How's that new phone of yours?" Jedi asked, typing commands into a nearby keyboard.

"Oh, um . . ." Sam stalled, before sheepishly confessing that he no longer had it. "It wasn't my fault this time—Hans' guys took it."

"Hmm, right," Jedi said, then went to a steel locker and rummaged noisily in the shelves. "I know I have something in here . . . somewhere . . ."

"I can get a new one at the airport," Sam replied, not wanting to add to Jedi's long list of things to do.

"Aha!" Jedi emerged from the locker and held out the largest, most ridiculous-looking mobile phone Sam had ever seen. It had a large black box connected to a phone via a spiral cord.

"That's . . ."

"*Awesome*, I know," Jedi said, plugging it in and switching it on. "Developed it as one of my first projects, when I was still a student at the Academy."

"What, in the 1900s?" Sam said, laughing.

"Very funny. I'm not that old."

"Seriously though, this is the size and weight of a phone book. In fact, I've seen phone *booths* smaller than this."

"I know—it's cool, right? It's totally retro hipster awesome. Everyone will be jealous of you with this baby held to your ear!" His eyes gleamed with genuine enthusiasm. "These were used for about five years by all Academy staff, but then discontinued because they were considered too dangerous."

"Dangerous, huh?" Sam said, looking closer at it. "What, its internal combustion engine was giving people headaches? Or microwaving their brains? Nuking their neural pathways?"

"Nothing of the sort," Jedi said, defensively. "It's the Swiss Army knife of phones, before smartphones. Here, put your thumb on the screen."

Sam did so and a light scanner flickered underneath it. The screen came up with chunky green text on a black screen.

`Welcome, Sam, to a new world of communications.`

"So the greeting is a little lame," Jedi said, fiddling with the controls.

"How does it know who I am?"

"It's tapped into the wireless network here."

"Nice. But I still don't see what's so dangerous about it."

"Only you can use it now," Jedi said, handing it gingerly to him. "I can handle it, because I'm the creator, but it still bites me sometimes."

"*Bites*?"

"Just a playful nip, nothing like what it'd give someone who you perceived as a threat."

"It—it can tell if an enemy picks it up?"

"Oh yeah, and a whole lot more . . ." Jedi ran through its

functions, very similar to Sam's last ultramodern phone. It was, indeed, an impressive handset, despite only just squeezing into Sam's backpack.

"So, you're heading out straightaway?" Jedi asked.

"To Brazil, first thing in the morning."

"Ah, Brazil . . ." Jedi's attention turned to his computer screen and he tapped in some commands. "Perfect timing! Can you hang around? I've got another surprise for you."

13

ALEX

Shiva walked away when the screen came alive and Alex leaned in closer for a better view. After a moment of fractured vision, the picture righted itself.

Finally.

"How you doin', Sam?" Alex said, fidgeting in his seat.

"Alex!" Sam said, as Jedi wheeled away to give them privacy to talk. "I'm doin' all right. Wow, it's good to see you!"

"I know, feels like forever, huh?" Alex said.

"How's things with you?" Sam asked.

"Yeah, I'm OK. It was a bit weird at first, you know, being away from you guys," Alex replied, "but it's actually kinda cool here. I got to see my mom again and I've been getting into the computer stuff."

"Right up your street, tech head!" Sam laughed.

"Totally!"

Sam cleared his throat. "I gotta say, I know what you did back in Berlin, at the zoo. I don't know how to thank you, saving me from Solaris and everything, I mean . . ."

Alex reddened. "There's nothing to say. You'd have done

the same thing. And one day you might need to."

"Very true, Alex. But I just wanted to say thanks."

"It's all good. But listen, I was—I was really sorry to hear about the attack at the Academy . . . I wish we had gotten a warning through sooner."

"Yeah. I know you guys tried to stop it," Sam said. "Everyone here is still pretty shook up about it. And then there was Pi . . ."

"Yeah, I heard. I'm so sorry," Alex said. There was a small silence between them. "And what about Eva? Is she OK?"

"She's fine. Took out a helicopter single-handedly during the attack."

"All right, Eva! Atta girl . . . I *knew* she was one tough cookie," Alex grinned.

"She really is. She'll be mad she didn't get to talk to you, though."

"Say hi for me, will ya?"

"I will," Sam promised, before adding, "so, any ideas about where Stella is now?"

"Nope," Alex replied. "Believe me, there's a lot of people here just itching for some payback when we do find her."

"And don't forget about Matrix," Jedi said, walking back up behind Sam. Adding, "Shiva, how's your setup going there?"

"A work in progress," Shiva replied, his face moving into the screen's frame next to Alex. "You?"

"About the same," Jedi said, looking at the mess of

computing gear surrounding them. "It's gonna be hard work going up against Matrix in this state. Take us another day or so to get some decent power running, and the better part of a week while we play catch-up."

"I hear you," Shiva replied. "But we're all working around the clock here."

"I've got the programming all sorted," Jedi explained. "I just need more hardware . . ."

"We've got that in spades," Shiva said. "It's the software I'm worried about. Matrix coded it all. I gotta ditch it otherwise he'll be able to get in and snoop around whenever he wants. At the moment I'm running on off-the-shelf tech. It won't take him too long to work that out and break in."

"You wanna link our systems?" Jedi asked.

"My thoughts exactly," Shiva replied.

"Just to find Stella, right?" Jedi qualified warily.

"Of course," Shiva said.

"Together we'd be much more of a match for Matrix," Jedi concluded. "I like it."

"Right," Sam said, seeing that the two tech heads were in agreement about cooperating. "You two can geek it out later. Alex, what are your plans?"

"How do you mean?" Alex asked.

"I mean, you want to come with me on my next trip?"

Alex smiled. "I'm listening. Where you headed?"

Alex could see Sam throw a look to Jedi, who nodded.

"The Amazon," Sam said. "Brazil."

"That's a big place," Alex said.

"Tell me about it . . ." Sam said. "We're still working on the exact location of the next Dreamer."

"I'd love to come," Alex said, smiling. He heard Shiva clear his throat with a little cough. "But I just have to talk to some people first. I'll get back to you asap . . . it's a little complicated."

"Sure thing," Sam said. "You'll need to get on it, though, if you're coming. We leave tomorrow."

14

SAM

Sam walked along a gravel path that circled around the school. He could see ordinary students in their dorms, the windows of the 18th century buildings lit up as they studied or talked or played games. He had been ordinary too, until just a few weeks ago.

And now this . . . no big deal, Sam, just the fate of the whole WORLD and all that.

Great.

He kicked a pebble off the path, watching it arc through the air and sail into a fountain with a gentle *plop.* He walked over and stopped by the fountain. A tall marble statue draped in robes stood in the center. The sun had set about half an hour earlier and there was a full moon casting reflected light that danced off the water and onto the stone face, making it seem alive.

"You're the one, Sam . . ." a deep voice said.

Sam spun around, but there was no one there.

"Only you can save us . . . you, and the other amazing students."

Sam spoke in a quiet voice, "What?"

"You are a greater god than me . . ."

"What the—?" Sam said.

Laughter erupted from the other side of the statue, and Eva emerged, saying in her mock-deep voice, "You are the only one who can save the world . . . no pressure!"

Sam laughed. "Yeah, great, thanks for helping me go even more nuts."

Eva stood next to him and they looked at the statue in silence.

"It's the Greek god Apollo," Eva said, "in charge of light and the sun, *and* prophecy . . ."

"Sounds like me," Sam joked.

Eva laughed.

"I mean, is that all he got, light and the sun?" Sam went on. "He had to be god of more than that, right?"

"Well, Apollo *was* the son of Zeus. And I think he got some wisdom and knowledge too."

"I wish *I* was the son of Zeus," Sam murmured.

"Why, so you could have even more to do?" Eva nudged him.

"Ha. Anyway, looking at this Apollo guy, he looks more like a wrestler."

"Funny you should mention that—they invented wrestling, the Greeks."

"Yeah, well, I *perfected* it, rah!" Sam said, wrapping an arm around Eva's shoulders and getting her into a playful headlock. "How will you get out of this?"

They wrestled, Eva twisting and turning to pull herself free. She leaned back and caught Sam off guard. They both tumbled over and landed on their backs, laughing, looking up at the stars above.

"So," Eva said, panting for breath. "I'm glad that at least you're still just a big jerk, and that being this Dreamer of the last 13 hasn't gone to your head." She paused. "Do you think Alex will be one?"

"I hope so. And you too. Well, kind of . . . if you know what I mean."

I'm the key to it all—it's my dreams that bring us together. I wish Eva would appear in my dreams, but I also don't want her to face the danger that comes with being one of the last 13.

Eva punched Sam playfully in the arm.

"Ouch."

"Just making sure you're awake," Eva said, "sleepyhead."

"Thanks," Sam said, rubbing his arm. "But next time, if my eyes are open, there's a good chance I'm awake."

"Ha, yeah, right, the amount of running around saving the world stuff you're doing, I wouldn't be surprised if you're sleep-talking to me right now."

She pinched Sam, hard.

"Ouch!" Sam said, getting to his feet and helping her to hers.

"OK," Eva said, "well maybe you really are awake . . ."

"Or maybe I'm a zombie!"

Sam chased her and she screamed out loud, running across the lawn, in and out of the shadows.

Sam sat on the end of Zara's bed, in the crowded dorm room she shared with Gabriella and Eva. Xavier was there too, reading a tablet as he lay on the floor. It felt almost normal for Sam, sitting there like that, talking and laughing for over an hour. They talked about dreams—about everything Sam and the others had seen out there, about what they missed, and what they didn't.

"Sam," Xavier said, "if you could go anywhere, where would it be?"

Sam thought about it for a while then said, "The moon."

"Huh?" Eva said. "Why, so you can see if it's really made of cheese?"

Sam threw a pillow across the room at her and said, "No. It's just that it's far away from here."

"And it's a place that you don't have to save?" Zara asked.

Sam shrugged.

"Less worry, I guess," Sam said.

"You are worried?" Gabriella piped up.

"I'm *always* worried," Sam sighed. "I mean, think of Brazil, tomorrow. What if there's no way of working out who the next Dreamer is? What if we end up just wandering around the Amazon, wasting time? Or, what if I do find him but we can't find the Gear? Or if Hans, Mac, or Stella and Solaris—or *all* of them—show up and crash the party again?"

"They're not crashing *my* party," Xavier said.

"Sam, you do not need to worry like that," Zara said, ignoring Xavier. Gabriella and Eva nodded. "You will be fine."

"It's a gift, Sam," Gabriella said. "We, but especially you, have an ability, to see into the future, that other people can only wish for."

"You just have to trust it," Eva added.

Sam nodded. There was a knock at the door, and Lora entered.

"Hey, lights out was twenty minutes ago," Lora said. "Guys, back to your rooms. It's a big day tomorrow, we need to be rested, OK?"

Well, at least I get my own room . . .

Sam's dorm room looked more like a closet than a bedroom. The bed was buried under a stack of rolled Academy posters, featuring famous Dreamers from years gone by. There were T-shirts, hats, and boxes everywhere. It looked like a storeroom for . . .

"Is this—Academy merchandise?" Sam asked.

"Sorry," Lora said. "The campus is overcrowded, and this

was the only room available with something that comes close to dream-recording connectivity."

Sam picked up a mug from a box on the floor. It had the Academy's emblem emblazoned on one side and a slogan on the other—*Sweet Dreams*. He pulled out a couple more from the box. One read *Don't let the bedbugs bite!*, the other, *What if all your dreams came true?*

"You guys serious with all this stuff?" Sam asked.

"I know, isn't it embarrassing?" Lora said, picking up a board game. "It was before my time, trust me. The former head of communications thought she had a flair for marketing—and had a grand plan that she was going to take the Academy public, make rock stars out of all of the Dreamers."

"Well, I'm sure glad she's not around anymore."

"She's around, but retired," Lora said. "She's my mother."

"Oops. Sorry, I, ah, didn't mean to be rude," Sam stammered.

"Please!" Lora grinned and rolled her eyes in mock horror. "You have no idea. You think this is bad, wait until you see her house. It is so full of this kind of stuff you can't turn around."

"And why didn't it happen?" Sam said. "I mean, going public . . ."

"Hard to say," Lora said, turning the board game over in her hands. "Probably because it's too unbelievable to the rest of the world. But Mom was determined. She never really did things by halves. Which is probably why she had my brother and me enrolled in archery and shooting clubs as well as cross-country skiing, lacrosse, soccer, underwater polo, karate, gymnastics . . . the list goes on and on."

"And I thought *I* had it tough here," Sam said, laughing as he cleared away all the rolled posters from his bed. He unrolled one, and nearly choked on his laugh when he saw the picture. "No way!"

"Oh, no!" Lora groaned, blushing.

"That's—it's you!" Sam said, looking at the picture of Lora in her Stealth Suit, standing side-on with crossed arms in a tough-guy action pose and a stern expression. "Ha!"

"I know! I was about your age. Or a bit younger, maybe about fourteen. Wow, can you believe my hair? I think I decided to go blond for the summer and, well, you can see the results."

"Yeah, your mother must *really* be nuts, letting you get that hairdo," Sam said, and Lora laughed. "Seriously, I think I'm gonna keep this. Show it to some of the students . . ."

"Don't you dare," Lora said, trying to look serious but not able to contain her smile. "Come on, it's getting late, let's get your dream recorder set up, just in case."

"OK," Sam said, serious once more. "I just hope I have the dream I need."

Sam woke and unplugged the dream cap, a much older version of what they'd had at the Swiss campus. Outside his window, the sun poked through clouds. It was just after seven and his stomach rumbled. He pulled on his Stealth Suit and headed downstairs, smiling to students as he passed.

Lora and Tobias were already waiting for him at a table in the dining hall. When he entered, a hush spread through the room, all conversations stopping simultaneously. Sam felt his face flush red with embarrassment as he sat down at the table.

"Carry on with your breakfast, please," Lora announced to the assembled students.

The murmur of conversation around the room slowly resumed. Many students kept stealing glances Sam's way.

Now I know how animals in the zoo feel . . .

Gabriella, Zara and Eva joined them with plates of food.

"How'd you sleep?" Eva asked anxiously, sitting next to Sam and putting her huge plate of fruit salad between them to share.

"I dreamed, but it was just the same as before. There was nothing new," Sam said, frustrated with himself. Xavier crashed down opposite him, holding two plates of bacon and eggs and toast.

"You looked like you could use this," Xavier smiled.

"Thanks."

"Jedi is decoding your dream now," Lora said. "He should have the results any minute."

"I don't think it will help. My dream was exactly the same, although I did see more of the name of the boat this time," Sam said, hopefully. "The Roosevelt-something."

"Ah!" Tobias said. "That's excellent, Sam. You're getting better at recalling details from your dreams."

Sam nodded as he ate.

Not good enough, though.

Sam ate a piece of bacon, thinking over what Tobias had said. He noticed Tobias' T-shirt—*I know a lot of jokes, but none about electricity. It's shocking.* He couldn't help but smile at the lame science joke.

"Well, I hardly slept at all," Xavier said. "I was researching with Tobias all night, working with Pablo—"

"From my dream?" Sam said.

"Yep," Xavier said. "He was searching through archives at the University of Brasilia. We worked with him through the night via video conference, trying to pinpoint that map in your dream—the one you found at the Vatican."

Sam asked, "Did you find anything?"

Xavier looked to Tobias, a glint of discovery in their eyes that shone through their tiredness.

"Oh, yes," Tobias said. "Show you after breakfast. We've got about three hours before we leave to catch our flight."

After breakfast, Sam and the others met in Jedi's computer lab, along with Lora and Tobias. There was anticipation in the air.

"Anything?" Sam had asked Jedi as soon as he walked in, hoping the replay of his dream would unearth more details than he could remember.

"Sorry, buddy," Jedi said, frustrated. "Everything replayed exactly as you had already described. Your level of recall is quite good, actually. Of course, if we had a more advanced machine here . . ."

"But we *do* have information on the map in your dream," Tobias continued, pointing to a large projection image of the ancient map on the wall. It was a simple diagram, the features of which looked like they were hastily drawn.

"Now, after going through many maps which contained similar features—"

"Thousands," Xavier interrupted.

"*Tens* of thousands," Jedi corrected, now brimming with pride. Sam thought it seemed like he was buzzing from drinking too many sodas.

"Yes, tens of thousands," Tobias said. "Working with Pablo, we think we've found the location of the map. It even matches up with some of the details from Sam's dream last night. Jedi?"

"Well," Jedi said, leaning back in his chair and enjoying the moment as everyone turned all their attention his way. "I'd like to point out that in the several hundred or so years since this map was drawn, the topography of the rivers and forests has changed significantly."

He clicked away at his computer and a satellite image was superimposed over the map.

"Ta-da!" Jedi said.

"It doesn't look anything like the map," Lora said, looking at it closely. "The rivers, the hills—"

"Here it is without the trees," Jedi said, bringing up a new image.

"Still looks nothing like the map," Sam said, seeing the rivers didn't match up. "I mean, maybe that mountain range matches up, but that's it."

"Well," Jedi said, "watch this, which I put together with Pablo using his university's data."

Sam and the others watched as the projected images went through a time lapse, back in time, in fifty-year increments. Sure enough, ten images later, the rivers matched up—*exactly*.

"This," Jedi said, "is the location of your map."

"Wait a sec," Sam said. "That's five hundred years we've gone back, isn't it?"

"Yes," Tobias replied.

"Then that's the right time frame?" Sam asked. "If da Vinci made the Gears we're looking for, that is?"

Jedi nodded as he brought up another, different map on the screen.

"This is a famous map called the Cantino Map, which we know dates from 1502," he said. "Our map's features bear a striking similarity to this one. We believe they were created around the same time and possibly by the same person."

"So you think da Vinci sent the Gear with some explorer halfway across the world?" Sam asked.

"Perhaps," Tobias said. "The dates would make sense."

"Cantino was not only an explorer," Jedi continued, "he was also suspected of being a spy for the Italians. Maybe he knew da Vinci."

"So the Gears somehow disappear around the globe," Xavier said, "and the last 13 find them through their dreams. Incredible."

"But we don't have much hope of finding this Gear unless I can see who the Dreamer is," Sam said, before adding hopefully, "are there any other leads from the map, or Pablo?"

"A few," Tobias said. "Cantino left a diary and in it he mentions meeting a local tribesman, someone from the Cloud People."

"They believed that Cantino's map would lead to a great treasure," Jedi added. "He just had to follow the clues to a city in the clouds."

"A city made of *gold*," Tobias went on, "the path to which is filled with danger according to the Cloud People."

"So what happened to Cantino and the treasure?" Sam asked.

"He went looking for it but never came back. We only have the remnants of the diary because one of his guides made it out of the jungle. He was raving with fever by then and no one's ever managed to piece together the information to find the city."

"So you think that *our* map will lead us to the city of gold and to the next Gear?" Sam asked as Jedi brought up a sketch from the explorer's diary.

"A needle in a haystack . . ." Eva said, looking at the current-day satellite image of the world, a blinking red dot of the location centered on the continent of South America.

"We've narrowed our search to Rondonia, a state in Brazil," Jedi said, bringing up another image on the screen.

"That's the boat from my dream!" Sam said.

"Rondonia was named after Candido Rondon," Tobias said nodding. "He was the last to search for this lost city on an expedition with Theodore Roosevelt. He came back empty-handed."

Sam studied the image of the ferry carefully, his eyes locking on the life bouy with *Roosevelt-Rondon* clearly stenciled around it.

"When was that expedition?" Sam asked.

"1913–14," Tobias replied.

"So," Lora said to Sam. "The map and the name of the boat have given us our starting point. Go to Brazil and meet Pablo. Take the ferry. You'll find the next Dreamer, Sam."

"And he'll find the Gear," Sam said. "And Stella?"

"Since you're now steering your dreams and are

conscious of them while you're dreaming, more and more new elements will creep in," Jedi said, "such as when you felt the ferry passengers watching you."

"Those dream quirks are obviously not going to happen in real life," Lora added, "and it sounds like you manifested Stella in your dream through your fear or anxiety."

"So she might not show up there?" Sam asked, silently willing them to give him the answer he wanted.

"Well, we can't say that for certain," Lora sighed. "But it is possible that she won't turn up, at least not as you foresaw it."

"We know that she has tapped into your dreams before, Matrix enabled her to do that somehow," Jedi said. "But even if she has, she can't know who the next Dreamer is if you don't. She may well think that we won't make a move until we know for sure."

16

RAPHA

Half a world away, fifteen-year-old Rapha Miguell was in his bedroom, a small space above a mechanic's garage, where he worked to earn his board.

He lay on his slim mattress and, like every night, he said good night to the photo of his parents and switched off the light, falling asleep listening to the sounds of the night outside his window.

RAPHA'S NIGHTMARE

The thrum of a powerful outboard motor echoes around us.

"You feeling OK?" I ask my companion. He looks about my age but taller, bigger than me in most ways. He's got sandy hair and clear blue eyes, and light skin as though he rarely sees the sun.

"Fine, thanks," he replies, catching his breath. "Thanks for pulling me out of the water."

"Your ferry sank?" I say.

"It was attacked," he says. "I'm Sam, by the way."

He holds out his hand to shake mine.

"Rapha."

We continue along in silence for a while, until the sound of a boat behind grows louder and louder. We both squint against the bright sun to see.

"Great," I sigh. "We have company."

Shouting, behind us. Then shooting into the air.

"No!" Sam says. "That will be Stella . . ."

The old junker of a putt-putt gets closer, belching out blue smoke and we can see there are five guys shouting furiously.

"OK . . ." Sam says, confused, "it's not who I thought. Friends of yours?"

"Ah, Sam," I say. "About this boat . . ."

"Yes?"

"Well, I, ah, technically, I don't really *own* a boat."

"Right . . ."

"Right," I continue, pushing the throttle full open. The engine sputters and then gives some extra power. "So I, well, I *borrowed* this boat."

Sam raises his eyebrows at me.

"*Borrowed*, *stole*, you know, just for a little bit. I left them a note though, saying it'd be back by tomorrow with a full tank of gas."

"And you think those angry-looking armed guys want it back about now?"

I nod. "I'd say so."

"Great," Sam says. "Well, let's hope you can make a high-speed getaway better than you can sneak away."

I give the boat everything its engine has—and it's clear that we are quicker than our pursuers, but not by much.

"Think they'll shoot at their own boat?" Sam asks as they level guns at us.

PING! PING! PING!

I do a double take and see that we're in the clear, as though time has skipped a beat. We are in the boat, floating through a village made up of wooden jetties with buildings on pylons, built around a tiny harbor. I am flooded with relief to see we are no longer being followed by our pursuers. I guide us through the throngs of tiny canoes and boats trading fruits and vegetables with the passing commercial traffic.

"There is my uncle," I say over my shoulder to Sam, pointing to where he stands on the jetty. "He'll hide this boat for us."

"Hide?"

"We will travel differently from here on," I explain.

Sam follows me along the rickety wooden passageway that winds its way through mazes of wooden buildings. Kids run around, laughing and playing games, joined by yappy little dogs.

"This way," I say, leading us onto land. Finally, in a clearing of jungle we come to a tiny dirt landing strip with a few tin-shack aircraft hangars.

"We're flying?" Sam asks me as we stop by the aircraft.

"Yes. Where we need to go is too far by boat—it would take us days."

"So we're going in *that?*"

"She's solid and true," I say. "She'll get us there in one piece."

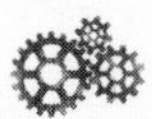

"My mother," I shout to Sam over my shoulder, the sound of the wind and the engine in my ears as we soar over the jungle below, "told me that some day you would come!"

"She was right!" Sam replies. "Are you sure you know where you're going?"

"Yes!" I reply, checking the fuel gauge—we're nearly on empty after a few hours of flying. "It's just up ahead!"

The little aircraft's engine fights for air as we climb, and heads straight into the white-gray of the cloud cover.

We burst through the clouds and the cliff face of the table-like mountain looms ahead of us.

"Pull up!" he shouts.

"I am!" I lean back on the control stick, the engine biting at the thin air as we climb higher.

"We're not gonna make it!" Sam yells.

I flick a switch behind my head and the engine roars with a new, louder intensity and we *just* make it over the lip of the mountain.

"Easy!" I say, laughing at the look on Sam's face.

"Rapha, you're either a genius or—"

CRUNCH!

We've hit something below!

"Hold on!" I say, fighting with the controls. I level out our flight. "Oh boy . . ."

"What?" Sam says.

The aircraft seems to be in perfect flight now. I dial the engine speed right back and we glide around in near silence.

"We've lost our landing gear," I say, looking under our seats.

"But—you can still land, right?"

"I'll try," I reply, though I don't feel confident. "We need somewhere nice and slick, with nothing to snag on which might make us tumble apart."

"Tumble apart?!"

I can see the top of the mountain is vast but made up of many differing types of vegetation—definitely a hostile landing.

"Down there!" I say, pointing down where the water rushes below. He sees nothing but thick foliage, but I know for sure now. It is here—at the waterfall.

"What's there?" Sam asks.

"Our landing site."

"What? Where, I don't see it."

We come in to land, hard, loud and too fast—

We are in a city. It is an old city, made of stone. We are atop the highest structure. I look around the ornate carving of the altar and marvel at its beauty.

"Where'd you get that?" Sam asks as he climbs to join me.

He points to a small brass gear in my hand.

"I found it, up here."

I twirl the mechanical-looking device in my hand, its toothed edges catching the dull sunlight through the clouds.

"We should go," Sam says. "I have a bad feeling that we're not alone."

Before we can climb down, I hear them. Then I see them. Hundreds, no *thousands*, of people materialize from nowhere and are climbing towards the altar where we stand. Warriors from a time long ago. We're trapped up here. They are yelling and screaming war cries as they charge.

In the middle of the swarming mass stands a man in black—he raises an arm to point at me. I cannot see his face.

Who is he? Why am I here?

I shrink away from the rushing crowds, swelling like an angry ocean.

They're coming for us.

17

ALEX

"How are you getting on?" Phoebe asked Alex as they walked down the hallway of the new Enterprise headquarters. "I feel like I hardly see you these days."

"I'm fine," he said. "I've been helping Shiva set up the computer systems here. Anyway, I like being in Amsterdam."

"You just focus on keeping yourself safe," Phoebe said.

"Yeah, right. Ah, Mom, I've been meaning to ask you something . . . I want to go out there, you know?"

"Out?" Phoebe stopped walking and turned to look at her son. "You mean out in the field? On a mission?"

Alex nodded. "With Sam. He's going to Brazil. I could help him."

His mother shook her head and looked sick with worry. "Not after last time. It's bad enough that Sam has to go," she said, "but he has no choice. You do. This is not an adventure, Alex, this is serious, and deadly."

"Well, what if I ask the director instead?" Alex challenged.

"He will agree with me," she said, now equally forceful. Then she added softly, "I'm sorry, Alex. It's just too dangerous. I won't let you go on your own again."

Alex could tell by the look in her eyes that it was useless to argue.

But why is it such a big deal? I'm not a kid anymore.

"Someone has to do it . . ." Alex said. "Why not me?"

They walked together in silence until Alex came to the door of the computer lab.

"I'll see you later," he mumbled, ducking through the door before she could reply.

Inside, Alex found Shiva had been up through the night, writing new layers of code to protect the Enterprise's computer systems. A few other techs wandered past, looking as disheveled as Shiva, mountains of fast food wrappers and drink bottles amassed in a corner. The room smelled of sweat and pizza.

"So, this is how nerds party," Alex said, trying to sound upbeat.

Shiva didn't respond, he just kept thundering away at his keyboard.

Alex said, "Right, what can I do?"

"How'd you sleep?" Shiva asked, still tapping away at new lines of code.

"Like a baby," Alex replied. "Though I can't even remember a moment of my dream."

"You're lucky," Shiva said. "You should see the dream waves from last night, check it out."

Shiva pointed at a large screen, which showed a map of the world, large red blotches over major city centers. Alex couldn't count the numbers that were being displayed—maybe half the world had had nightmares the previous night.

"Each of those represents the severe nightmares experienced last night," Shiva explained. "It's a touch screen, so feel free to tap on it to get more data."

Alex touched on the patch around Los Angeles.

"Over a million nightmares?" Alex said, seeing the bar graph showing types of dreams broken down into categories. "You're able to measure the entire population's dreams?"

"Not quite," Shiva explained, putting his feet up on a desk and sucking at a straw in a huge cup of cola. "It's kinda like TV ratings."

"Huh?"

"We've got a certain number of Dreamers who plug into dream recording devices, then we extrapolate that data to represent the city or town as a whole."

"Right . . ." Alex said, tapping on San Francisco, then Mexico City, Rio de Janeiro and Brisbane. "I'm guessing these kinds of numbers aren't normal?"

"They're so far from normal it's insane," Shiva said. "You can read the previous stats on those tabs below—it'll take you back week by week."

Alex did so, and watched as the screen changed each couple of seconds to smaller and smaller bubbles of red—going back a year, the red clouds were nothing more than tiny dots at the world's largest cities.

"So what does this mean?" Alex asked.

"It means the Dreamscape is being seriously affected by what is happening. More and more people are subconsciously aware that difficult times are approaching."

"What can we do to change it?"

"Win the race," Shiva said. "If Solaris or Stella get the Bakhu machine up and running? Well . . . that will lead them to the Dream Gate—and if they get to *that* first? I think it's safe to say that we'll *all* be enjoying nightmares after that. I mean, who knows *what* kind of sleeping and waking world we'll find ourselves in, should they open the Gate and get the power that lies beyond."

"Great," Alex said. "And you and I are stuck here, watching it happen."

Shiva smiled and said, "Speak for yourself. It's not all writing code and desk jockeying around here."

"Oh?"

"You underestimate the Great Shiva, my friend."

"You're the *Great* Shiva now?" Alex said. "I'm so not calling you that."

Shiva laughed.

"But, wait, what are you saying—there is something we can do from here, on our computers, about all these nightmares?"

"Oh, yeah," Shiva replied. "Strap yourself into a chair, and watch and learn, my friend."

18

SAM

Sam flipped the Academy's jujitsu instructor onto his back and the guy landed with a *thump!* Sam swiftly followed up with a compliance hold. The instructor broke out of his hold and flipped Sam onto his back.

"Yield!" Sam called after he knew he was pinned. "I yield!"

"You're getting better," the instructor said, letting go.

"Nice," Sam said, getting helped up. "Again."

The two of them weaved around each other. Out of the corner of his eye, Sam saw that Lora and Eva had come into the dojo. His attention was momentarily distracted and the instructor easily flipped Sam onto his back again.

"Argh!" Sam got to his feet and went back to his position. The instructor looked ready to pounce.

"Think you can take two of us?" Lora called.

"Bring it," Sam said, without looking at her—he knew she was still well out of reach, and he moved to his left, opening up the floor and getting them both in his sights.

The instructor rushed at him. Sam sidestepped and tried a flip which was parried and redirected to flip him. Sam rolled over the instructor's back, turning the instructor inside out from his previous stance.

Lora rushed at him, but with her dart gun drawn. Sam, interlocking his elbows through those of the instructor's, dropped with all his weight and turned forward into a roll, flipping the instructor over his head—

THUMP!

The instructor knocked Lora over and the two of them tangled on the floor in a heap. Sam was already standing, triumphant, with Lora's dart gun now in hand.

"OK," the instructor said, catching his breath and laughing. "He's ready."

Outside, Sam walked with Eva, following Lora through the maze of school buildings and then across the sports fields. He thought they were headed for the boathouse but then they took a path towards the woods. The path led to a clearing which Sam could see was an archery range.

"Something for you," Lora said, handing Sam her dart gun. "You might need one of these."

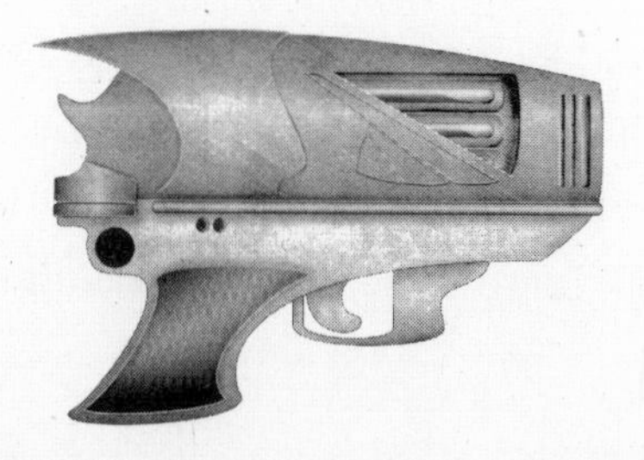

"Really?" Sam said, holding the weapon.

"It's like any other air pistol," Lora said, "only it fires small darts, about an inch long."

Sam felt the weight of the weapon in his hand.

"The darts are tipped with a neurotoxin," Lora said, "that will shut down a target for anywhere from half an hour up to about six."

Sam nodded, remembering Sebastian shooting him in the neck, close-up and hitting him mid-vein . . . he'd dropped like a sack and was out for a few hours.

"The length of time they're out will depend on their size and physiology, as well as where you shoot them, but even the biggest guy, shot in the back, will be incapacitated for thirty minutes." Lora pointed to the top of the pistol grip near Sam's thumb. "There's a setting there to adjust the levels."

Sam asked, "How many darts does it hold?"

"Eighteen," Lora replied, and handed him two more loaded clips. "And there's enough compressed gas in there to go through nine clips, then you have to change the cylinder."

Lora demonstrated by pulling the gun apart in a couple of seconds, then piecing it back together in a series of clicks.

"I don't think I'll get *that* trigger happy," Sam replied, testing out the loading sequence.

"Go ahead," Lora said. "Send some darts down the range."

Sam aimed the weapon and fired—it hit low.

He tried again, on the level but to the right.

"Try and be steady with the way you pull the trigger," Lora suggested. "Squeeze it gently."

Sam did as instructed—still far wide of the bull's-eye. He fired another three times, getting closer to the center target each time. Then he tried a few combinations of quick-drawing in different stances, and got the hang of it when he finally hit a round next to the bull's-eye.

"Good work," Lora said. "I sometimes forget what a quick learner you are."

"Thanks," Sam said. "Eva, want a shot?"

Eva's eyes narrowed.

"I'm not really a fan of weapons," she replied.

"Come on . . ." Sam said. "One shot."

"It might come in handy one day," Lora encouraged.

"Fine," Eva replied, taking the dart gun. She took aim and squeezed the trigger.

WHACK!

"That's—incredible!" Sam said, marveling at the small dart stuck perfectly in the middle of the tiny target. Eva raised one eyebrow and handed the dart gun back to Sam.

Lora's phone beeped. She was still smiling as she read the incoming message.

"I've got to run back, but you should stay and practice. Finish those clips then replace the gas canister," Lora said, walking away.

Sam fired off the remainder of the darts and then loaded in a new set.

"Come on, you know you want to see if you can do that again," Sam said, handing the dart gun to Eva again. She smiled and took it from him. It looked big in her hands. "I mean, anyone can get lucky once, right? But can you do it again?"

Her dart hit the bull's-eye—right next to her first, and far better than any Sam had fired. She laughed and fired a couple more times, both projectiles hitting close to the previous ones.

"I think you'll find the answer to your question is yes," Eva said, handing the gun over. "Last year I was first in Washington State under 16's in archery."

Sam smiled and shook his head as he unloaded the gun. "You are a girl of many talents, Eva."

"Yes, Sam, I am," she grinned.

They walked slowly towards the helicopter pad.

"Are you scared?" Eva asked. "I mean, about going out there again?"

"A little bit," Sam admitted. "My dream . . . it was so weird. And, well, you'd think I'd be used to seeing myself like that. But this whole new dream-steering thing that messes with what's real? *That's* scary stuff."

"You know what," Eva said, staring absently at the ground as they walked, "you should do one thing every day that scares you."

"Sounds like good advice."

"It is," Eva said.

"Where'd you get that from?" Sam asked.

"My mom used to say it."

The sun poked through the low dark clouds and the dew on the grass shone like crystals.

"There's something else, isn't there?" Eva said and Sam was conscious that she was interrogating him. "Was it your dream? Something that you aren't telling me?"

"No, I promise, it's not that."

"What then?" she persisted.

"I just hate saying good-bye to you guys," Sam said. "Especially after what happened at the Swiss campus. I should be here, with you."

Eva pointed at a squad of armed Guardians walking the perimeter of the forest.

"We'll be fine here, don't worry about anything other than yourself," Eva said. "Those aren't dart guns *they're* carrying. Not anymore. Besides, someone has to keep things running behind the scenes." She nudged him gently.

Sam nodded. They rounded the corner of a building and saw that the helicopter was readying for takeoff. Tobias and Xavier walked over to it with their packs slung across their shoulders.

"But will *you* be OK?" Sam asked.

Eva looked across at Sam and for a few seconds there was silence between them.

"You're the one who sees so much more of the future than me," she said. "So, you tell me—*will* I be OK here?"

"Yeah," Sam said, smiling. "I think you'll be fine."

"We're leaving!" Tobias called from the helicopter as the rotors started up. "Your bag is on board already, Sam."

Lora joined them, and Sam could tell that she had some news to share.

"We've found Mac," she said, "or rather, he's found us. He wants to meet."

"He does?" Sam scoffed.

Lora nodded, then said, "I'll go straightaway. Eva, you up for a field trip?"

"For sure."

"Good, we'll leave now, too."

"Don't forget what Mac tried to pull on us in France," Sam said. His face creased with concern. "You guys will be careful, won't you?"

"Don't worry—we'll find out what he's up to and what he wants," Lora said. "He said the situation is not how it appears. And it would be better to form some kind of truce with him, to work together if we can, than have him as another enemy. At least for now."

Sam nodded doubtfully, looking back to the chopper. They were ready for takeoff, now just waiting for him.

Eva hugged Sam, who strapped his pack on tight.

"Be careful out there," Sam said to her.

"We'll be OK. You've seen me shoot," she said with

another grin. "You just focus on what you need to do. Just remember to breathe. Come on, Lora, we'll be fronting Mac long before these guys get to Brazil. Let's roll!"

Sam waved good-bye and smiled a bittersweet smile as he ran to the chopper. "That's *my* catchphrase."

19

EVA

"Is it your first time in Chicago?" Lora asked.

"Yes," Eva replied, walking behind four hulking Guardians, "and I can see why they call it the Windy City."

"I know, this is pretty extreme, even from what I've seen over the years," Lora said, as they made their way across the forecourt of the Willis Tower. "It's just up here."

Inside the lobby, shadowed by Guardians, they took the elevator to the eighty-second floor, where they met a group of police officers and several FBI agents. Eva watched as Lora spoke to the senior officers and agents.

A few moments later, she came back over.

"They're keen to talk to Mac," Lora said. "They want to ask him some questions about what happened in Paris. According to his message, sent by an intermediary, he's due to be here today. His office is a few floors above us."

"And then what?" Eva asked. "They'll move in and arrest him for what he did to the Dreamer Councillors?"

"Possibly . . . we don't have any hard evidence about what happened in Paris," Lora replied, "so it's more of a line of inquiry at this point."

"But what about the way he confronted Sam?" Eva persisted.

"That might have been unpleasant, but you can't arrest someone for that. He didn't actually do anything to Sam or Zara. Tempting as it is to paint him as the bad guy, what we really need is to find out what he's been up to and who he's working for—or with."

How come she looks so uneasy, then?

"Well, I'm glad you let me come," Eva said decidedly. "It's time I got more involved."

"I'm still not completely convinced you should be out in the field with me," Lora cautioned, then she gave in and smiled. "But I figure you've earned your place in all this and besides, I like us working as a team."

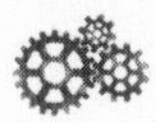

"Subject entering the building," crackled the police radio in the setup room of the Chicago skyscraper.

"Finally," Eva said to Lora, and the two of them stood and watched the surveillance footage of Mac entering the lobby of the building and waiting for the elevator. He had four bodyguards with him.

"I say we go in as soon as he gets into his office," a captain from the Chicago police said. He had two squads of heavily armed SWAT members waiting on the fire stairs, out of sight and ready to roll.

"No," Lora said. "I'll go in, try talking to him first. I want to hear what he has to say, and then I'll tell him he's surrounded. I don't want this to end up getting ugly if we can avoid it."

The cop nodded, and all in the room turned to watch the flickering image of Mac in the elevator, rising up to his office.

We've got all the backup we could need. So why do I feel so nervous?

SAM

Sam had never been to South America, and after London he wasn't prepared for the heat and humidity as he stepped out of the air-conditioned plane. The lush palm trees behind the chain-link fences of the airport runway on the outskirts of Brasilia gave it an instant tropical feel. They walked to the terminal where—thanks to Tobias and his Academy paperwork—they breezed through customs and out into the street. The sights and sounds and smells of another world hit Sam's senses all at once.

"I'm getting us some of that grilled corn," Sam said, sniffing the barbecued goodness in the air, "and some cold drinks."

"Right behind you," Tobias said. "Make mine a double—that airplane food was terrible."

"Wait up a sec, guys," Xavier said, as they zigzagged across the busy road of honking cars, trucks and motorbikes all shuffling along in some kind of well-organized chaos. "Do we have to worry about snakes around here? In the jungle or whatever, I mean?"

"Snakes?" Sam said, waiting in line for the food vendor. He blinked in the brightness of the sky, so very different from that which he'd last seen in England.

"Yeah, snakes," Xavier said, looking at him wide-eyed. "You know, slithery, slippery, sneaky, *poisonous* things."

"Nah," Sam replied, smiling to Tobias. "The snakes here, well, let's just say I wouldn't worry about the poisonous ones."

"Oh?" Xavier said, visibly a little relieved.

"Oh, no," Sam said. "It's just the ones that will swallow you whole that I'd worry about."

"Yeah," Tobias said, cottoning on to the joke. "That's right. The big snakes here will eat you in one big ugly gulp."

"Right . . ." Xavier said, turning pale.

"Don't worry," Sam said. "The spiders ate most of the snakes. Didn't you do any reading up on Brazil on the flight?"

"Nope . . . just how big are these spiders?" Xavier said.

Tobias nodded and spread his hands wide to show how big they grew in these parts.

"*Serious*?" Xavier said.

"Yep," Sam said, paying for the corn. "That big, and hairy too, *huge* fangs."

"Oh boy . . ." Xavier had turned white and looked like he'd lost any appetite he may have had.

"It's fine, don't worry about it," Tobias said to Xavier. "Like the snakes, it's not that these giant spiders are really poisonous, it's just that they might take your arm or leg off with a single bite."

Xavier shuddered as Sam and Tobias burst out laughing.

Just then Sam heard their names being called, and spotted Pablo waving at them across the road. They crossed over to the shade of a huge tree, where Pablo stood by a white four-wheel drive. Two other vehicles full of Guardians were parked close-by. Here, the huge guys who looked after Dreamers were in military-style uniforms with their weapons out in the open.

Different country, different rules, I guess. Don't know if seeing them like this makes me feel more or less safe.

"Welcome, it's such an honor to be joining you in this race," Pablo said, shaking their hands. His jolly stomach and bald head were wet with sweat. "Ah, Tobias my old friend. Xavier, how wonderful to meet you, I'm a longtime admirer of your father's work on the Council. And Sam, you are a wonder, to be certain. Now, are we all ready for an Amazonian adventure?"

In Pablo's office at the university, Sam sat at a large table along with Xavier and Tobias. The eight Guardians who had shadowed them there from the airport remained outside in the hall, along with a couple of security guards watching the entrances.

"You're safe here," Pablo said, sensing Sam's wariness. "Thanks to the Professor pulling some strings with the government, this university has a small private army of security guards on hand."

Sam nodded.

"Here," Pablo said, passing a package to Xavier. "It arrived in the mail a few days ago."

The package was still sealed.

Xavier pulled open the paper wrapping to reveal a small leather-bound journal, with maybe a hundred pages of scrawled, tiny handwriting and diagrams inside.

"That's it," Xavier said. "Wait, there's a note," he added. "Oh. It's for you, Sam." He passed it over and Sam read it aloud for everyone.

Dear Sam,

It was good to have met you in Cairo. I have noticed since your visit that I am being watched, and I fear that I will soon be taken in by forces that oppose us, for they will want to find out all I know about this dreaming lore.
I will stall them as much as I can, but that may not be enough to ensure you beat them. Everything I know of this quest that is important and relevant, is noted here in this journal. Study it closely, for you'll need it to keep your head. Best of luck to you and Xavier, and the rest of the last 13, for what lies ahead.

Your friend, Dr. Ahmed Kader

"I wonder why he addressed the package to me, then?" Xavier puzzled.

"Perhaps he thought that was safer than using Sam's name," Tobias said.

"So we need to get everything we can out of this journal," Xavier said, flicking through the pages of scrawled notes and drawings. "Luckily I've been around his terrible handwriting my entire life, otherwise we'd be in big trouble."

"Can we scan the journal?" Tobias asked, looking at the pages. "That way we can enlarge the pages on the computer, and work on them simultaneously here and back at the Academy."

"I can get that underway at once," Pablo replied, and picked up his phone and called for his assistants.

He turned back to them as he hung up the phone. "Is there any further news on Dr. Kader's whereabouts?" he asked.

"I'm afraid not," Tobias said. "We've put together a small team through the Council of Dreamers to search for him. But our resources are so stretched at the moment, there's not much else we can do."

"My father told me that the Egyptian police have alerted international authorities to keep a look out for him," Xavier added sadly.

"He might have gotten spooked and gone into hiding, fearing that he was about to be abducted. Or . . ." Tobias trailed off.

"Or those who were watching him may have taken him," Sam said, finishing Tobias' thought.

"Like Hans or Mac?" Xavier asked.

Tobias nodded. "They may have him, or, like I said, with any luck he decided to go into hiding and he may just plan to stay hidden until this is all over, helping us out from the shadows."

"Kinda like you did out on that mountain," Sam said.

Tobias smiled.

"It's such a pity," Pablo said. "Kader would be such a brilliant man to have with us for this kind of mission."

"We'll have to make do with what he left us in this book," Sam said. There was a knock at the door and Pablo ushered in two of his academic assistants who immediately went to a computer and began diligently scanning the journal's pages.

"Good luck reading some of his handwriting," Xavier said. "When I was a kid, he used to make treasure maps for me to follow and find chocolate in his workshop. They were so bad neither he nor I could find half the loot he'd stashed. To this day I still find candy from ten years ago on dusty shelves and under his relics."

Sam and the others laughed at the image of decade-old candy bars squirreled away among Ahmed's library of priceless artifacts.

"Yeah," Sam said, "well, fortunately it's the next Dreamer who will lead us in the search now, not your godfather."

"Perhaps," Pablo said, "but I take from that note you read out that Dr. Kader knew of some details in your quest ahead that will require a little, shall we say . . . *careful* reading."

"So we know where to go, to the ferry," Sam said, looking at a computerized map that showed the *Roosevelt-Rondon* marked at its mooring. It was due to be there in six hours. "I wonder what's so important about Ahmed's journal?"

"Well, I've been taking a look," Xavier said, "and there are some diagrams in there, including how to overcome booby traps . . ."

"OK, that *is* handy," Sam said, studying the intricate drawings made from decades of research by Dr. Kader. "What's this?"

"It looks familiar," Xavier said, staring at the image on the next page.

"It's a field tower," Pablo chimed in. "Part of a dream machine they built in the 1930s and 40s, based on earlier designs by Tesla."

"Nikola Tesla was one of our most famous Dreamers. He had astonishing vision and created incredible inventions," Tobias said. "The towers were originally designed by him to generate energy, and to transmit that energy either through the ground or the air."

"Wireless energy," Sam said with a sideways smirk to Xavier. "Remember doing that earlier this year in class?"

"Yeah, I remember," Xavier said. "Man, that old science teacher we had—remember all those lame ties he'd wear?"

"Very amusing, boys," Tobias laughed, shrugging off their joke. "But these towers were assembled in locations around the world by the precursor to the Enterprise."

"When it was a government operation?" Sam asked.

"That's right," Tobias replied. "It was called Bureau 13 then. Mac used to work for them. He was their last director before they shut the program down."

"Man, how old is this Mac guy?" Xavier asked.

"Old, but still very capable," Tobias said. "Anyway, they installed these Tesla towers around the globe and listed them as special generators for telegraph communications. But they were really put in certain places around the world to tap into the Dreamscape."

"The emphasis is on 'were,'" Pablo said. "They were all dismantled when the program ended."

Tobias countered, saying, "I heard there is still one in the Ukraine that was too contaminated to dismantle. And the prototypes are still located in Tesla's old workshop in Manhattan."

"They would be under thick layers of dust and rust by now," Pablo said. "Inoperable."

"Maybe. There are some variations of dream readers still active in public spaces," Tobias said, "like our own in the Eiffel Tower. And there are several monuments and buildings around the world that have the devices hardwired in, switched off but still able to be activated some day."

"Why'd they shut it all down?" Sam asked. "I mean, I understand them putting a stop to what Bureau 13 was doing with the human experiments and creating Dreamers, but why switch off all these Dreamscape recorders? Wouldn't it be useful for us? I mean scientifically, to collect all that data over the years, to better understand how and why we dream, to better see what we are capable of?"

Pablo was smiling, and he said, "You are very astute, Sam. And yes, this has been an argument for a long time. But it comes down to privacy. Who is to say if we are allowed to see into everyone's dreams?"

"And who's to say what happens if someone else taps into it?" Tobias said. "That's the real danger, and why the program was shut down. *And* why this race to get to the Dream Gate is so vital for us to win. Imagine if someone not only had the power to look into everyone's dreams—imagine if they could *control* them."

"Did someone try before?" Xavier asked. "Is that why the Department 13 or whatever got shut down?"

"Yes, only it was *after* they disbanded the Bureau, by some rogue scientists of Mac's," Tobias said. "In America, at a place called Three Mile Island, they tried to power up and switch on the world's biggest dream antenna, hooked up to several skyscrapers in the city. It would have tapped into the dreams of the entire eastern half of the United States, right up to the Rockies."

"But it failed," Sam said. "You taught us about that meltdown in class, right?"

"That's right," Tobias said. "The scientists defected to Russia, and a few years later tried the same thing there."

"And failed again," Xavier said.

"I'm guessing you also learned what happened at Chernobyl," Pablo said. "Tobias has taught you boys well. And now you know the truth of those meltdowns. *This* is what caused it—they were in over their heads, it never should have been allowed."

"Times were different then," Tobias said. "Russia and America were two great powers pitted against one another, each wanting the ability to affect a nation's dreams, to see everyone's secrets. But they never understood that the power of the dream world is too much for us to control like that."

"What did they do?" Sam said. "These field towers?"

"They read dreams, among other things . . . but they didn't work, at least not on the scale envisaged," Tobias said. "Tesla's original concept was for a special power field to be tapped into, firstly in the ground, and then in the atmosphere."

"Huh?" Xavier said.

"He wanted to turn the atmosphere into a conduit for electricity," Tobias said. "That didn't happen, so Bureau 13 bought up all the devices and searched for other power sources that were big enough to tune into the Dreamscape. One was placed at Hoover Dam—even that didn't work."

"How about in Brazil?" Sam said, tapping Dr. Kader's notebook. "Did Tesla ever set up towers here?"

"Not that we've ever heard," Pablo said. "But it's been my life's work studying dreams in this country, and there are amazing stories from survivors of mass, shared nightmares during the 20th century."

"Who was doing all these experiments?" Sam asked.

"The director of Bureau 13. A man named Louis, but they called him the Dream Catcher."

"Is he still around?" Sam said.

The two men were silent. They looked to Xavier.

"No," Xavier said, stunned, as though he'd been hit by a

bus. "But his son is. And his grandson."

"Who's that?" Sam asked.

"Dr. Dark's father," Tobias said. "Louis was his father."

"And my grandfather," Xavier said. "I had no idea. I knew he was a successful scientist, that he spent his last days working in the Ukraine . . . I wonder why my father never told me."

"He's probably ashamed of it," Tobias said. "As brilliant a man as your grandfather was, he was out of his depth. He dared to dream as big as he could, but he overreached."

"It's OK," Sam said, putting his hand on Xavier's shoulder and looking his friend in the eyes to try and reassure him. "We've been in the, well, *dark*, about a lot of things."

Xavier smiled at the reference to his name.

"There'll be time to learn more, from your father," Sam said, then checked his watch. "But right now, we've got this journal to work through and a ferry to catch."

"These descriptions in the journal match the map," Pablo said, pointing at the big-screen image of pages from Dr. Kader's journal. It had been nearly two hours of painstaking reading, with Sam and Xavier tackling the first fifty pages and Pablo and Tobias the next.

"The river mentioned, the River of Doubt, matches up with descriptions of rapids and waterfalls, here, and here,"

Pablo said. He pointed at the map. "There may well be more descriptions of the entrance to the city, but we are unsure."

"Where'd Dr. Kader get this information?" Tobias asked.

"He's an Egyptologist at heart, but I know he had a bit of a da Vinci interest on the side," Xavier said. "His life's work is studying antiquity, but even with all the Egyptian stuff, he has always had a passion for the Renaissance."

"What's that?" Sam said, inspecting the sketch that Dr. Kader had made.

"Looks like hopscotch," Xavier replied.

Pablo got closer to the screen to make out the scrawled handwriting. "It looks like it's a description of the booby traps at the entrance to the Cloud City." He turned to look at them all in wonder. "Could it be?"

Then the Guardians burst through the door.

"All right," Tobias said, having conferred with one of the Guardians. "Stella was sighted in Brazil, a few hours ago. She's got a couple of teams of rogue Agents with her. But she's disappeared again—she could be anywhere now."

"We should split up," Sam said straightaway, "and break up into a couple of teams ourselves. You guys," he motioned to Tobias and Xavier, "go with the Guardians to the east, and make a lot of noise about it so that one or both of her teams pursue you. Meanwhile, Pablo and I will get to the ferry and meet the Dreamer."

Tobias nodded and said, "Good idea."

"We'll take the journal with us," Sam said to Pablo. "And Tobias and Xavier, when you get back here, keep analyzing the scanned copies and all the information we have."

Pablo nodded but Xavier looked unsure.

"Pablo and I go alone," Sam said, adjusting his dart gun in his hip holster, then picking up his backpack. "That was the dream—and having the two of you make a diversion, that'll help us change things up, cool? And if she does catch up with us, then we'll change it some more. I'll go with the Dreamer and use the journal to search for the Gear while Pablo keeps leading the chase away from us."

Xavier finally seemed to agree.

"Wait," Pablo said, looking surprised. "You mean we go now?"

Sam smiled. "No time like the present."

"But I haven't even packed . . ."

"I know how you feel," Sam said with a smile.

Sam and Pablo's first leg of the expedition was in a seaplane that flew them up to the river in the city of Porto Velho. Pablo seemed either ill from the flight or by the suddenness of it all. Sam felt saddened during the flight when he saw great swathes of dense green forest cleared to smoldering orange-brown mud, making way for cattle.

People got to eat, I suppose . . .

The set down on the water felt like riding a skipping stone, and as they climbed from the aircraft, Sam put his backpack over his shoulders and helped Pablo up onto the jetty. The academic might well have been an expert in the history of his country, but he was no fieldman, a fact his brand-new safari-type outfit attested to—as well as the trouble he had walking across the uneven planks of the jetty.

Great, imagine if we land in trouble on the ferry.

"That's it," Sam said, pointing over at the ferry named the *Roosevelt-Rondon*. A big vessel, it was exactly like in his dream, painted pale yellow with blue window frames and with four tiers of decks. There were large paddles at the side and rear to propel the boat along the brown river.

"Then let's get ourselves some tickets," Pablo said.

The paddleboat cast off and began its gentle sway up the Amazon River. On board, Pablo settled into a chair in the diner where assorted trays of high tea were amassed. He continued to read through the journal while Sam familiarized himself with the boat. There were two dining compartments, one on the large main deck, and one on the top level that served more as a noisy bar full of commuters, drinking and playing cards and dice games as the river passed underneath them. Sam calculated there were maybe two hundred people aboard spread out over the upper decks, the lower deck taken up with cargo and livestock.

Out on the rear deck, Sam watched as other watercraft chugged by. He scanned the faces, hoping one would be familiar from his nightmare. His phone rang. It was Tobias.

"Hi," Sam said.

"Hey," Tobias replied. "Where are you guys?"

"On the ferry," Sam replied. "About half an hour in."

"Keep your eyes peeled," Tobias said. "We just had word that Hans and his German Guardians touched down in Peru."

"Peru?"

"He's coming at you from the other side."

Great. That changes things . . .

"How would he know where we are headed?" Sam asked.

"Now *that's* a million-dollar question," Tobias said.

"Maybe from Dr. Kader, if they have him captive?"

"Maybe, but the timing is too suspicious," Tobias sighed.

"It's like he knows where I am right from when I first arrive," Sam said.

"Exactly."

Sam was silent, then said, "How does he do it?"

"If we can't get rid of him for good, we're going to have to somehow flush out his source of information."

"You think it could be someone back at the Academy?"

"Maybe. We'll see. Meantime, we're tracking your location and we've sourced two helicopters so Xavier and I will be able to get to you within a couple of hours if need be."

"Any sign of Stella?"

"Yeah," Tobias laughed. "They're about a hundred miles from us, stuck answering questions from the local police after we tipped them off that they were a group of poachers."

"Nice! That should buy us some time."

"My thoughts exactly," he said. "Good luck," Tobias said as he hung up.

Sam gazed out at the river behind them. "Come on, Dreamer, where are you?"

ALEX

"Ready, 'Thor'?" Shiva asked.

"When you are, Shiva," Alex replied.

"Go!"

From the comfort of a couple of large beanbags, wearing their wraparound visors, they entered the playing field of the latest first-person shooter game, hunting down an enemy as a two-man team. Shiva was awesome with his shots—"one shot, one kill," he liked to say while playing, while Alex preferred to blaze away on full auto and take his chances that he'd always manage to reload before getting blasted out of the game.

"So, let me get this straight," Alex said. "You've coded this game so that each bad guy we take out is actually a nightmare being destroyed in the Dreamscape?"

"Yep," Shiva said, tossing a grenade into a room full of targets.

"This seems like too much fun to be doing something actually useful and life-changing in the real world!"

"I've linked all the bogeys in the game space to the different types of nightmares that we're coming across in this local area," Shiva explained. "And don't worry, the fun will wear off when you see the hordes that are marching against us as the nightmares grow and multiply."

"You should get others recruited into this," Alex said.

"The whole world is playing against the nightmares," Shiva replied. "They just don't know it."

"Huh?" Alex pulled off his visor to stare at Shiva.

"I've managed to code a whole bunch of games and link it to the world system of gaming consoles, via Jedi's supercomputer."

"So people all around the world, right now, are playing their regular 'shoot 'em up' console games on the Internet, and all the while your program is running in the background?"

"Yep!"

"That is *so* unbelievably awesome, but I have no idea how you even thought of it—let alone did it."

"What's *really* cool is how I patched it into the electronic waves that our Dream Towers around the globe tap into—genius thinking, right?"

"Absolutely, man. I'm totally blown away." Alex pulled his visor back on and adjusted his sight, shooting a couple of bad guys out of a window at the top of a building.

"Just don't get blown away in here," Shiva said.

"Thanks, I won't," Alex said, as their avatars regrouped behind a shipping container, reloading and patching themselves up. "There's a team headed for us, eight of them."

"On it," Shiva said, moving his guy into position. "Thirty seconds."

"Backing you up," Alex said. "So, how's this 'changing people's dreams via computer games' work exactly—via electro what?"

"How long you got?" Shiva grinned.

"I got all night, man," Alex replied. "Top right!"

"Got him. Well, OK, let's see . . ." Shiva said, as his avatar broke from cover and Alex mirrored his moves, crouching behind obstacles and laying cover fire while Shiva moved to a better vantage point. He started to shoot sniper fire at the attacking force. "What you have to first understand is that we are all energy, and that our minds are all operating at certain wavelengths . . ."

"Ah, Shiva?" Alex said.

"Yeah, Thor?" Shiva replied, switching to a rocket launcher to take out an attack helicopter that had kept them hunkered down behind a crane at the city's docks.

"You hear that?" Alex asked.

"That rumbling?"

"Yep."

"I thought it was the chopper," Shiva said.

"The one you just ditched into the bay as a flaming wreck? A dozen people will have a sound sleep tonight because of that and they thank you, I'm sure," Alex said. "But no, I hear something else."

"Yeah, me too . . ."

Their avatars looked around in every direction, but aside from the carnage they'd wreaked, there was nothing to see.

"What *is* that sound?" Alex said, exasperated.

"I've got an idea," Shiva said. He took a moment to flick through his inventory and then produced a small model plane. "Launching a UAV to give us eyes in the sky."

The little aircraft was thrown into the air like a paper plane, and then its propeller took the aircraft soaring high into the sky.

"You can patch into its view to see it on one side of your visor," Shiva suggested.

"Got it," Alex said.

Shiva took the aircraft up and started circling it overhead, overseeing their two guys standing on the docks, waiting. From that height, they could see the full extent of the destruction of the city by the nightmare troops. There was also the path that they and the other gamers had carved through the terrible landscape.

At least the destruction is just in the game space. But the nightmares people must be having to create this . . . man.

"Ah, Thor, you see what I see?" Shiva interrupted Alex's thoughts.

"I think so, but I don't know what I'm looking at . . ." Alex said, watching as what appeared like an entire city block moved towards them.

"Flying in for a closer look," Shiva said and the little UAV in the sky zoomed down fast to get a closer look at it.

"Is that . . ?" Alex began.

"A tank?"

"That's no ordinary tank," Alex said.

This machine was a monster—the treads at either side were the size of the houses that it was driving over. The barrel sticking out the central turret was bigger than several smaller ones combined. And at the sides were smaller turrets with nasty looking add-ons.

"That's *the* tank," Shiva said. "And I know who created it and sent it at us."

Alex's heart sank. "Matrix?"

"You bet your butt. All right, if we're going to take him down, we need to use our heads as well as our bullets."

24

SAM

Two hours in and still no sign of the Dreamer.

Sam paced and watched.

Or anyone else who's after me, or him . . . at least that's good.

When the ferry slowed and pulled into another stop, a group of men came aboard. They were clearly not typical passengers. Sam was on the crowded top deck, and watched as the five of them, dressed in serious-looking gear and reflective sunglass, scanned the crowds.

Could just be actual adventure tourists, or undercover cops. Or they could be connected to Hans or Stella.

Sam rushed down two decks and found Pablo working on deciphering a riddle in Dr. Kader's journal.

"Ah, Sam, there you are," he said without looking up from the book. "I do think that I've nearly—"

"No time! A group of guys has just gotten on and I think they may be—" Sam stopped when he clocked them across the room, at the far side, some fifty people between them. They hadn't seen him yet. But *he'd* seen *them* and he now *knew* they were trouble. Under the jacket of the guy in the lead, Sam could make out the distinctive shape of a dart gun. "Come on!"

Sam half dragged Pablo to his feet and they made for the rear deck, two levels below. The ferry was underway once more, the pier now a long way behind them—too far to swim for it without being picked off.

And who knows how fast Pablo can swim? Are there piranhas or 'gators down there?

"Sam, what do we do?" Pablo asked.

Sam snapped out of his thoughts. There were a couple of lifeboats up along the midsection of the ferry.

"Head for those," Sam said, pointing, but then he saw two of the men below, searching for them.

They saw him and drew Enterprise dart pistols.

Well, I know who they are now—Stella's goons. And I know that they're not here to kill me. They want me alive, no doubt to tell them who the next Dreamer is.

"This way!" Sam said, leading Pablo to the very back of the boat, where below them was the large paddle that provided the forward momentum of the boat. There was an opening before it, part of the cargo bay or engine compartment, which they could climb down to.

"I can't make it down there," Pablo said, tucking the journal into Sam's pack. "I'll hold them off, you go!"

Sam had no choice—they were getting close, the other three converging from the stairs leading from the deck above. He pulled his dart pistol and fired at the first two, hitting one, who slumped back, while the second ducked for cover.

Eva would have hit them both . . .

It took a moment for those on the ferry to react, but when they did, they became a human tidal wave, pulling away from Sam and Pablo, dozens of passengers fleeing and heading towards Stella's men, effectively stalling them a little.

"Go!" Pablo said. "And don't look back, not for an instant!"

Sam passed him the pistol and climbed over the handrail, carefully hanging down, not wanting to fall back onto the massive churning paddle wheel. His fingers slid off the rail, wet with the spray—

Sam fell.

25

So this is what it's like to be inside a washing machine on spin cycle.

Sam's world was a war zone—all noise and commotion underwater, the water a mess of bubbles and vortexes. He couldn't see but tried to relax and go with the currents that pushed him down fast between the paddle and the back of the boat. It felt like he spiraled downward forever, his lungs burning.

When the pressure lessened he kept his body still, and felt the boat disappearing. Turning towards the sunlight above, he saw the surface and kicked his way up, breathing out the last of his air as he rose.

"Argh!" he gasped as he broke the surface and sucked in air. The ferry was already paddling down the river. He couldn't make out Pablo on the back deck, but before he could wonder what had become of him the sound of a boat's engine came thundering upon him. He turned—

Too late.

When Sam came to, all he saw was gray sky. His senses slowly came back, one by one. He could tell he was lying on a hard surface and heard an engine roar in the background. The thick heady scent of the Amazon River was still in the air. The taste of the muddy water was in his mouth, making him sit up to cough it out.

"Aha, you're awake," a voice said. "I am Rapha. You are safe now."

Sam was on a long speedboat. The side of his body he'd been lying on was all asleep, as though he'd been out of it and lying still for a long time. He turned to face the voice.

It belonged to a lean and wiry teenager with dark skin and thick black hair twisted into dreadlocks.

"It's *you!*" Sam said, getting up to his knees and gingerly making his way over. He couldn't contain his happiness. "But . . . how? How'd you find me?"

Rapha eased off the engine's throttle and eyed Sam with a spooked expression.

He said, "Do you know me? I don't think we've ever met."

Sam took a deep breath. "My name is Sam and we have met before," he hesitated before plowing on, "in a dream." He looked expectantly at the boy but his face was impossible to read. "You dreamed to be here, at the ferry, to save me, didn't you?"

"Yes, it's true," Rapha said. "I dreamed of rescuing you from flames, then I woke up—but later, when I slept again, the dream changed. I saw you in trouble still, here on the river, but this time without the fire. I almost didn't come, but it was a feeling that I could not shake. I followed the ferry, and then there you were, floating face up behind it. Did you dive from the boat?"

"Yeah, something like that," Sam said. "Thank you, so much."

"Sem problemas," Rapha murmured as he turned the boat in a wide arc to travel back the way they'd just come. "I just can't believe I found you—and from my *dream!* I knew that I had to get you before . . . before something else did."

"Something?" Sam asked.

"A black figure, a fire demon."

"Solaris," Sam said, a shiver running up his spine. "His name is Solaris and he's not good news."

"I believe it," Rapha agreed.

"What else did you see, in your dream?" Sam asked.

"A place," Rapha replied. "We were flying up into the cloud-covered mountains. We're searching for something there, yes?"

"Do you know what?" Sam continued.

Rapha nodded. "Some kind of disk or something, gold maybe, with teeth—mechanical."

Sam smiled. "Yep. We need to find a Gear."

Rapha nodded but was silent for a while, motoring the sleek little old wooden boat along the river.

"What is it?" Sam asked.

"My parents . . ." Rapha said. "That's why I came today.

They told me that some day I might have a dream where I would see what it was that I had to do. They told me that this might happen."

"Where are they?" Sam asked.

"They—they were killed," he replied, tears in his eyes.

"When?" Sam said, wary. Rapha looked like he was about to fall apart.

"A while ago," Rapha said, "in an accident. But the last thing they told me was that I would meet someone who I had to follow, who . . ." He scrubbed his eyes and composed himself. "They said it was my destiny to meet this person, and to follow my dreams," he managed.

"That's right," Sam nodded. "It's very good to meet you, Rapha. And it's not just your destiny—it's *ours*."

Rapha and Sam spent the rest of the journey back down the river sharing their respective dreams in as much detail as they could recall and twenty minutes later they came to a fork in the river system.

"We will go to my place, we can take the ultralight," Rapha said.

Sam nodded then felt ill at ease. He couldn't place his dread at first, until he heard a sound.

PING!

A bullet ricocheted off the steering assembly between them.

Behind their craft, a big boat full of—

"It's the smugglers!" Rapha said, pushing the throttle of their boat forward to get to full speed.

"The what?" Sam asked. He looked back and quickly realized they were no smugglers—they were rogue Agents.

Just like those from the ferry.

"I dreamed about them too!" Rapha said.

"Anything else you need to tell me about your dream?"

Sam said, gripping on to the side of the boat as Rapha wheeled it around wildly.

"That's about it! But look in that case under there by your feet."

"If you've got some fancy driving skills, now's the time to go for it," Sam said, reaching down for the case in the bottom of the boat—

"Oh yeah!"

Sam was on one knee and pointed the flare gun at their pursuers. Rapha was now pushing their boat to its limits. The gun was an old-style launcher, the wooden handle chipped and worn. Sam lined up his target and pulled the trigger.

The projectile was in the air as he reloaded from a box of shells—

BOOM!

It sparked and shone bright orange as it hit the water.

The Agents escaped the first round, but Sam was reloading and aiming again.

Rapha turned the wheel hard to evade some gunfire that stitched up the river just where they'd been.

SPLASH! SPLASH! SPLASH!

Sam tipped over, firing as he fell. The flare shot high up into the air, almost straight up.

"No!" Sam said, losing the round in the sky.

"They're going to kill us!" Rapha screamed as Sam scrambled to his feet.

"No, they're not," Sam said, looking around, seeing a big sandy bank dead ahead. "They're trying to steer us towards that beach to have us trapped."

Bullets hit the side of their boat.

THUD! THUD! THUD!

A whistling noise cut through the sound of the boat's engine.

The bright burning flare was hurtling back to earth.

Sam couldn't see it—but the Agents must have. As one, a dozen men jumped off their boat and into the river as the flare smacked down right into the middle of their boat—and right into a canister of ammunition.

KLAP-BOOM!

The huge fireball made bits of boat rain down, splashing into the river all around them.

"Nice shot!" Rapha shouted out, grinning.

Sam joined him at the wheel as Rapha eased slightly off the throttle. They left the Agents swimming to shore.

"How far is it to your place?" Sam asked.

"It's around the next bend," Rapha said, looking up at the sky. "And with any luck, we'll have clear skies for our flight."

27

It was raining heavily as Sam and Rapha flew above the Amazon rain forest. Sam craned his neck to take in the astonishing views all around them. The swaying green sea of the tree canopy revealed flashes of the rain forest underneath—giant tree trunks, crisscrossed with vines, scurrying creatures on the forest floor and countless insects that fluttered and squeaked. There was the sparkle of the winding river while exotic birds filled the air with their color and echoing songs.

Sam saw a panther break out into a run across a clearing, hurtling towards a group of animals at the river's edge. He leaned over to watch but it was too far—the two-seater ultralight plane wobbled dangerously and Rapha pulled him back with a grin.

The plane was basically an open buggy with a hang glider wing above and an engine strapped to the back driving a propeller. The sound of the motor behind them was deafening.

"You know where we're going, right?" Sam yelled across to Rapha.

"There!" Rapha said, pointing ahead.

Out of the clouds emerged the cliff face of a table-like mountain soaring out of the jungle.

"Pull up!" Sam said, but he didn't need to, as Rapha pulled back on the stick and increased the engine speed into the climb.

"It's fine!" Rapha called. "The top of the mountain is not much beyond this cloud cover."

Sam gave a thumbs-up but failed to even reassure himself.

"In my dream," Rapha shouted, "the mountain was high, looming just beyond the clouds."

"*Beyond* the clouds?" Sam replied.

"Here we go!" Rapha said, and suddenly—

They were in a world of gray, flying in the middle of the dense cloud. The rain had stopped but the moisture in the air coated them immediately. Sam's clothes were soaked through and his goggles were splattered with water. They were now flying completely blind, relying on Rapha's memory and skill along with the GPS coordinates on the tiny screen between their knees.

"Five seconds!" Rapha said.

Sam held his breath as they continued their climb, waiting to break through the dense layer of cloud at any moment . . .

Five seconds came and went, then ten, then twenty.

How big is this cloud?

"OK!" Rapha shouted, leveling out and tapping the GPS. "We're definitely over the mountain's edge."

"You're sure?"

"Altitude reader on this says so."

"But the clouds . . ."

"Looks like it's going to stay this way!" Rapha yelled.

Sam looked down. On his side there was nothing but gray. Gray below, gray above, gray all around.

"How are we going to land in this?" he asked.

"That is, well, that is a good question," Rapha said, looking down tapping the GPS, and then facing Sam. "And I don't have a good answer."

They flew in silence for near on five minutes, in which time Sam's gut filled with growing dread. *What if the cloud cover is like this all day? Do we fly around until we're forced to land blind for lack of fuel?*

"Truth is," Rapha said, "there are nearly always clouds covering these mountains."

"You knew that going in?"

Rapha nodded.

"Have you flown here before?"

"Couple of times," Rapha replied. "Not quite this far into the west though. Just along the edges. The warmer ocean winds from the other side of the mountains make for dangerous flying."

"Do you know where you're going?" Sam asked, wondering if he dared hear the answer. "You know the waterfall—from your dream?"

"Yes, of course," Rapha said. "I've mapped the GPS of the waterfall. Just another thirty miles."

Sam saw on the speedometer that they were doing about eighty miles per hour, which meant about twenty-five more minutes in the air. He tried to relax.

Rapha seems relaxed and he knows what he's doing.

"Relax," Rapha said intuitively. "We're well above the level of—"

There was a *WHOOSH* under them and Rapha pulled back on the stick and pushed the throttle open, taking them higher in altitude.

"Some trees are tall around here, though," Rapha explained, with what sounded like a nervous laugh.

Sam swallowed hard and nodded.

"This area belongs to the people known as the Chachapoyas, the Warriors of the Clouds," Rapha said, adopting the tone of a tour guide. "They live in the cloud forests of the Amazon, which is now part of Peru."

"They're still there?" Sam asked, amazed.

"I wish it were so . . . maybe their descendants are still there," Rapha said, starting to slowly take the aircraft down. "The Incas conquered their civilization just before the Spanish arrived in Peru. The local legend says a large group of the Chachapoyas escaped and went east. They're the ones who built the fortress city we're heading for."

"Have you seen it?"

"The waterfall yes, the lost city no," Rapha said, cutting the engine right back so that they were now in a quiet, gliding flight.

"Hence it being a 'lost' city."

"Right. No one in living memory has seen it. There are only mentions of it, like in that journal of yours. But it's not like that is the only such place—all the time they're discovering more massive ruins in remote, heavily forested areas of the Amazon."

"It's more than a big jungle, then," Sam mused.

"Oh, yes!" Pablo said, animated by the notion. "It was inhabited for centuries by peoples who lived in harmony with it. Now, I fear, in recent times, we are seeing hard times for the Amazon rain forest."

"Yet somehow," Sam said, after a moment of quiet, peaceful gliding, "about five hundred years ago an explorer stumbled across this lost cloud city and made mention of it in a journal."

"Yes—look there!"

Ahead, the sky was getting brighter, until—

They shot out into clear sky, the low banks of clouds behind them and a clear blue sky all around.

"There!" Sam said, pointing ahead.

Down below, a few miles ahead of them, an enormous waterfall seemingly spewed out the side of the mountain range that formed the highest peak as far as the eye could see.

"That's it!" Rapha said. "Lucky for us this is the worst year of drought in this area—the waterfall's usually more than twice as strong."

Sam couldn't imagine that. The waterfall literally shot out from a hole in the mountain and once gravity exerted its influence, the water cascaded straight down, far clear of the cliffs behind.

"Now, we just need a clear place to set down . . ." Rapha said.

"What about there?" Sam said, pointing to a muddy landslide near the left bank of the river created at the foot of the waterfall.

"Maybe," Rapha said, "let's go around first and take a better look."

He banked the ultralight around, away from the mountainous cliff face, then circled back towards the water. At their current altitude, they were level with the top of the waterfall.

"What's that?" Sam said, pointing around halfway down.

"Let's get closer," Rapha said, lowering the aircraft and buzzing past an outcrop revealed by the retreated, drought-affected waterfall.

"Are those . . ?"

"Yes," Rapha said as they flew right by five tall stone statues depicting people. "They're Chachapoyan . . . and I just found our place to land."

28

Sam had to close his eyes for the landing approach. Rapha had done another circling arc to bring the ultralight towards the statues, only this time he was so close to the cliff face that Sam felt he could reach out and touch it. Ahead, in front of the statues but behind the curtain of water, there was a ledge about twenty feet wide.

"I've seen these in a newspaper photo," Rapha said. "But it's no entrance to a lost city, otherwise I would have read about that, I'm sure!"

"So what do we do?" Sam asked.

"Set down and take a look," Rapha said.

"You're serious?" Sam said.

"Saves us climbing the cliff under the waterfall," Rapha replied. He was silent as he powered right down and glided to a slow landing.

The ground was as hard as it looked. As soon as they made contact with the ledge, Rapha yanked on a lever that sent out a grappling hook that bounced and jangled along as they bounced in their seats—finally snagging against the rocky ground and pulling them to a violent halt, just inches from the edge of the ledge.

"OK . . ." Sam said. "That was the second scariest thing I've ever done."

"The second?! What was the first?" Rapha asked, gathering his breath back. He shut off the engine and closed the fuel line.

"You know, after the last couple of weeks," Sam replied, taking off his helmet and climbing out of the plane, "I'd have to think about that."

Sam looked down and saw the ground underfoot was actually a smooth, cobbled surface like an ancient road, worn with centuries of use, yet it was so well constructed that no grass or weeds could grow in the microscopic joins between the stones. When Sam walked up to the statues, he found they were over twice as tall as him.

"Come, Sam! See this," Rapha called, squeezing behind the statues.

"What have you . . ." Sam trailed off as he looked, stunned, at a hidden plateau behind the statues. "Man, you'd never know all this was here from the air."

"I guess it explains how they got the statues up here," Rapha laughed, looking out at the wall of forest. "The trees must screen this meadow."

"But where to now?" Sam said. He searched the back of the statues but couldn't see anything revealing in the rock face behind them.

"When we landed, I think I saw something," Rapha said,

leading the way around a slight curve in the face of rock past the last statue. The scrub cleared to flat stony ground, the carvings in the rock as intricate as a mosaic.

"This is it," Rapha said, pulling a headlamp flashlight from his pack to illuminate a stone-lined archway built into a natural cave formation behind the waterfall. "*This* is the entrance to the city."

They looked at each other silently as Sam slipped on a headlamp and switched it on. Inside the cave, the stone floor continued until the cave narrowed to a tunnel that seemed too well-formed to be natural.

People have been here. The Cloud People?

"The waterfall must have hidden this," Sam said. "We're lucky we came when it wasn't so full—we might never have seen this."

"Yes, I think you are right," Rapha said. "Let us see where it goes."

"Wait," Sam replied. "Careful where you step."

Rapha looked from Sam to the tunnel floor. Etchings in the rock showed scenes of hunting and war, telling some ancient story in the stone. "In case we wreck the archaeology?"

Sam shook his head and said, "In case we trigger a booby trap."

Rapha nodded and led on, slowly, carefully choosing his footing. A few times he paused and backtracked, walking around a carving that looked too ominous, watching out for a hidden mechanism that might trigger a terrible trap.

But no traps were triggered and after a while Sam felt as though all the notes in Ahmed's journal were not going to be needed.

They followed the tunnel as it twisted and turned its way through the rock of the mountains, coming into a room that opened up to a round chamber. An *empty* round chamber.

"It's a dead end," Rapha said after several minutes of searching.

"No, it's not . . ." Sam said, flicking through the pages of the journal. "I've seen this somewhere . . . here, see!" Sam pointed to a drawing. "And the note shows that it's here that we 'ascend to the entrance.'"

"Ascend?" Rapha raised his eyebrows.

"We climb?" Sam said, shining his light upward. The flashlight beam was lost in the inky black above. The two of them again searched the room with their flashlights, this time looking up.

"Maybe this *was* it, once, a long time ago," Rapha said as he walked back in Sam's direction. "A tomb or something, and whatever was here has been taken. Or maybe there was a rope ladder that's rotted away?"

"Or maybe not . . ." Sam replied. In a wall before him was another mosaic carved into the stone. What made this stand out was that it was the only part of the wall that was decorated.

"Here," Sam said, looking at the journal, and then the

carving. "Can you read this?"

"It's a pictogram," Rapha said. "These are stairs, these are . . . guards?"

"Ahmed's notes say we ascend beyond the guards," Sam said.

"So—what, beyond this wall?" Rapha asked. "Or maybe it's not a wall at all . . ." he said, inspecting every bump and seam in the rock before him. "Maybe it's a . . . door."

Rapha pressed a carved rock.

CLONK!

Just like Zara, his dream is showing us where to go.

The wall slid back, just a few inches and then they pushed against it with all their strength. Big enough now to squeeze through, the opening revealed a narrow stone staircase, encased in centuries of dirt and dust.

"Ergh!" Rapha said, lifting his feet from thick gloop splattered all over the floor. "Bats?"

"Well," Sam said, passing by. "At least we know there's a way out if bats can get in here."

The stairs spiraled up the sides of the chamber into the black nothingness above.

"Looks like we have a bit of a climb ahead of us," Sam said.

"I'm right behind you!" Rapha said, muttering under his breath. "I really don't like bats . . ."

EVA

Eva's hands shook as she watched the monitor, seeing Lora walk out of the elevator and into the lobby on the office floor where Mac was waiting. As Lora moved into the office's reception area, the security footage switched to the tiny cameras the police had mounted in secret the night before, the resolution grainy and unclear. She watched as Lora was patted down by the bodyguards and was shown into Mac's office.

"She's in," the police captain said into the radio. "All teams confirm ready."

The speaker on the desk relayed the radio replies of the police teams:

"North exit, copy that, ready to move."

"East exit, copy that."

"South ready."

"West exit, ready to roll."

Eva turned to the four Guardians in the room.

"I'm getting the jitters," she said to the nearest one. "I can't watch."

"It'll be fine," he replied in Russian-accented English.

"She's one of the best Academy graduates I've ever seen. Smart and fast."

"Here she goes, look," another Guardian said.

Eva watched as Lora walked across the room to Mac.

"Why's there no sound?" Eva asked.

"Tech issue," a cop replied. "We're workin' on it."

Eva felt sick at the thought of something already going wrong—and then, she saw Lora do a double take, looking quickly around the room, then back to Mac.

". . . wrong guy."

"Sound's back on," the captain said.

Eva leaned in closer to the speaker and the screen.

"You're telling me that you didn't attack the Councillors in Paris?" Lora continued.

"That's right," Mac said.

There was a pause, then Lora said, "And that's why you called this meeting—to set the record straight?"

"Yes."

"Can you prove it? That it was not you, or that the attack was not ordered by you?"

"Yes."

Lora paused again, waiting for more. When he said nothing, she asked, "Well? Prove it, or you'll be arrested on suspicion of the attack and questioned by the police."

"Yes," Mac said. He continued to just stand there, behind his desk, resolute as Lora walked right up to him—

"Something's not right!" the Russian Guardian said.

Then, Eva watched as Lora grabbed at Mac's face and seemed to pull at it.

"What the . . ." Eva said, looking closer at the screen.

Then, Lora stood on the desk and held something up to the camera's lens.

"What is that?" Eva said.

"A mask," the police captain said after ordering his teams into the office. "Mac gave us the slip somewhere and sent in a phony."

"He's buying time," Eva said. "He wanted us tied up here on a wild-goose chase. But why?" Eva looked at the guy under the mask as police rushed the room. He was confused and frightened at what was happening.

I hope it's not because Mac is out there making a play for Sam.

SAM

"The stairs end here," Sam said, nearly slipping off the wet stone underfoot and falling back into the void. He looked back down the dark chamber. The drop to the stone floor would be enough to kill and the stairs were slippery. "Watch your step."

"OK. Any bats?"

"No."

Ahead, the landing turned a corner and funneled into another tunnel. Sam led, always wary for anything that might be a trap and realizing that it was likely impossible that they'd see one until it was too late, for everything was made from the same gray stone, the finish impossibly smooth. They walked out into the tunnel, where the ceiling curved into an arch. The walls bore pick marks from their excavation out of the solid rock.

"Stop!" Rapha called. "The floor!"

"What is it?" Sam asked. He froze and looked down to his feet. The stones here were irregular in shape but they still fitted neatly into one another. It was almost as though instead of being carved and fitted together they'd been *melted* together—some had four or five sides, others had ten or twelve, yet somehow they all slotted together like a tightly packed jigsaw.

"This part of the floor is different from the rest of the cobbles," Rapha said. "Larger, for one thing. And look closer, some are a bit lower than others."

"But these ones are higher than the surrounding stones," Sam said. "And . . . they have *carvings* on them. Monkeys, jaguars—"

"Birds, snakes . . ." Rapha continued. "Bats."

"I've seen this before," Sam said, taking Dr. Kader's journal from his pack. "Here, look."

"The way the tiles are notated in here, it's like the whole hallway is a hopscotch game," Sam said. He shone the flashlight on a section of floor ahead that had disappeared, now only an ominous gaping hole. "Only this is no game. You step on the wrong piece, it's game over—for good," he said.

"Your Dr. Kader must have pieced this together from records left by the survivor."

"Yeah. He only survived for a few days after being found at a settlement, but the map was made from the story he told before he died," Sam continued. "And that helped spawn the legend of the lost city of gold."

"El Dorado . . ." Rapha shone his flashlight over the symbols and looked back to the drawing in the journal. "It's very similar to the stones before us. Pretty clear recall from a guy on his death bed."

Sam paused, then said, "You think that he was delirious?"

"He had the fever," Rapha said. "I've seen what it can do."

Sam looked again at the floor, and then the diagram.

"I think we've got no choice but to trust this book," Sam said.

"I just hope he remembered the right tile."

"Yeah," Sam said, then he read from the journal. "Look, it says here, stick to the single monkey figures only."

They stood and traced the route ahead—an easy step from one to another, although there was an area near the end, about ten yards away, near the black area where the floor had dropped out, where they could not see a monkey carving.

"I'll go first," Sam said. He pulled his backpack's straps tighter, slipping the journal into his pocket. He stood rock still. Thinking . . . waiting.

"Sam?" Rapha nudged.

"Yeah, yeah, I'm going," he said, taking some settling breaths. "I mean—it doesn't say what happens if you get it wrong. What do you think would happen?"

"Perhaps don't think about it is the best advice?" Rapha said.

"Right."

"I mean, maybe the floor will drop out from under you," Rapha offered.

"Awesome. Yeah, I think I preferred the 'don't think about it' bit." Sam paused longer, relaxed as much as he could. He lifted his leg and set off, reaching out with a long step to the first monkey tile. He tested it gently but it remained strong underfoot, with no movement at all. He brought his other foot to it and they just fit, blotting out the tile. "OK, so far so good."

Sam made his way with a wide stride to his left. Overbalancing, he shot out his right foot which landed on another monkey tile next to it.

"Phew, that was lucky," Sam said, trying to plot the way ahead.

"It does make me wonder," Rapha called out, now at the first tile. "What happens if we step on another carved figure . . ."

Sam stopped and stared down at the area ahead, just before the section that was missing.

"What is it?" Rapha asked.

"There's a group of tiles up ahead that are all covered over in bat droppings," Sam replied. He crouched down, all his weight on his monkey piece of the floor tile. He shone his flashlight along the surface. "I can't make out any of the markings at all—it's all just dark and slimy."

"Can you jump to the other side?" Rapha asked, shining his light ahead. "Land just there, before where the floor has disappeared."

"Maybe," Sam replied. *It'll be close . . .*

"And don't stop," Rapha said, his flashlight piercing the darkness ahead. "That patch where the floor has given out, that's the end, so you make it over that, we've got this licked."

"Licked?"

Rapha shrugged. "Heard it in a movie once."

"You're enjoying this now, aren't you?"

"Beats getting shot at on the river."

'Even if there's bats?"

"Where?!"

"I'm just saying."

"Or," Rapha said, looking back to where they'd started, "we could go back and find something to clean the tiles off with, so we can see what they are?"

"No, I think I can make it," Sam said, visualizing the

leap in his mind. He practiced his launch a couple of times, then leaning back on his heels for momentum, he pushed off, leaping forward.

Sam just made it to the other side of the moss. His feet skidded on the damp cobbles on the other side, causing him to slide towards a six-foot section of missing ground.

He jumped again—

And landed in a tumble that ended when he spread out his arms and legs and stopped himself against a wall. He got to his feet, dusted himself off, then turned back to face Rapha, smiling.

"Piece of cake. Your turn."

"OK . . ." Rapha said, although he looked spooked. He tried a different approach, going *back* two monkey pavers, readying himself, then he ran and jumped—

One tile.

Two.

He made his final leap.

The back of his foot landed just short of the end of the moss, making an ominous *CLICK* as his weight rested on a different tile.

"*Jump!*" Sam yelled.

In one fluid movement, Rapha bent and sprung forward, arms outstretched as he threw himself through the air.

Sam lunged forward, grabbing the front of Rapha's shirt and pulling Rapha towards him as—

A stone wall thundered down from a recessed slit in the

ceiling, smashing the grimy section of tiles and sending out showers of dust.

Sam and Rapha covered their faces and coughed in the settling dust.

"That was—"

"Close," Sam said. "Too close."

"We're trapped," Rapha sighed, staring at the wall behind them.

"No, we're not," Sam said, determination in his voice, looking away from the wall. "We're just not going out this way. Come on, we have to keep moving."

31

ALEX

"That's everything I got," Shiva said, running over to where Alex was taking cover behind a tower of big steel shipping containers.

"I'm down to my last med-pack," Alex said. The game had gone from a fun way of beating nightmares to a nightmare in itself. Try as he might, Alex just didn't see that they could get beyond this boss of a tank. He was tired and thirsty, and his hands were aching from the controls.

"Me too."

"That tank must have a weakness . . ."

"No," Shiva replied. "That, my friend, is Matrix. I'd know his game play anywhere. He wouldn't allow any weakness in the design. We just have to keep at him. Coordinate more players to come to our aid."

Alex scanned around 360 degrees and saw that while there were some individuals and small groups of players joining in the fight, they were falling thick and fast.

"Matrix always did like to showboat by being the biggest and baddest dude on the block," Shiva said.

Alex felt stupid, sitting there under cover, waiting until this tank found their final hiding place on this pier in the shipyards.

When that happens . . . we lose. We lose, that tank rumbles on, keeping the real world plagued by nightmares.

"So, what happens when we die in this game?" Alex asked. "Tonight, I mean?"

"A bad night for about a hundred thousand people," Shiva replied. "I just hope that the other players attacking his flanks have some kind of brain wave to get him neutralized."

"So what can we do?" Alex said.

"We can be a decoy to distract some of his guns," Shiva said. "Buy our buddies a little time, that's about it."

"Great . . ." Alex's avatar used the magnification of his sniper rifle's scope to zoom in on a huge container ship tied up to the pier, half-unloaded. If they were seen getting onto that, they'd be sitting ducks for Matrix's main gun, which he'd already seen turn a platoon of good guys into a crater the size of a city block. The only other thing on the dock was the massive overhead crane that moved the shipping containers on and off ships.

The crane . . .

"Shiva, call me crazy—"

"You're crazy."

"Ha, yeah, but you see that crane behind us?"

Shiva said, "Yeah?"

"I think I just . . . yep," Alex said, hope in his voice. "I did—I just had an idea that I know you're going to like!"

32

SAM

"Sam," Rapha said, his voice full of awe. "I do not think that we are in Kansas anymore."

"You sure do like your movies . . ." Sam said. His voice trailed off as they emerged up a final flight of stairs onto a stone podium, four columns soaring above to what might, five hundred years ago, have been a thatched roof. Now it, like the rest of the roofs on the thirty or so structures around them, was long gone. The result was a vast maze of stone buildings, covered by the canopy of giant trees, their upper reaches consumed in an ever-present layer of low, thick cloud. Sam could make out a wall, like a cliff, that curved around the entire space. "I think we're inside an old volcano."

"And that is why this has not been seen from overhead," Rapha said. "We are in a basin that is always clouded over."

"It's incredible . . ." Sam said.

They made their way down twenty or so slippery stone stairs to a courtyard filled with oddly shaped totems carved with similar animal reliefs as the entrance hall floor. Sam watched his footing but found that the ground appeared to be solid stone, flat as a concrete parking lot. As they walked on, he saw plants and flowers that looked unlike any he'd ever seen before.

"Now I feel like we're *in* a movie—a sci-fi one," Sam said. Before them, pillars of ancient wood stood as towering sentinels. Beyond them stretched hundreds of such pillars, some waist height, others taller than a two-story house.

"This must have been a prehistoric forest," Rapha explained. "Maybe the volcano was dormant for a few hundred years, maybe longer. The trees grew in here, then it flooded with lava one day. Covered by silt and sediment, they survived when everything else eroded, leaving this. I've heard of a similar thing before."

"Where?" Sam asked.

"A *long* way from here . . ." Rapha said. "Or, at least it looks like it."

"What do you mean?"

"This place reminds me of a place my father told me he'd seen as a boy, Mount Roraima, at the border with Venezuela. It was 'found' by the English explorer Sir Walter Raleigh in the late 1500s. Here, close to the border with Peru, we're a long way away."

"Well, this place was found by Europeans around that time too," Sam said. "But do you think it has remained untouched for the last five hundred years?"

"Yes, I believe it's possible."

"What a mind trip . . ." Sam said. "Exploring where no

one's been for hundreds of years. I'll really have to introduce you to Zara when we get out of here," he smiled, thinking of how they had discovered da Vinci's hidden workshop.

Rapha pointed, said, "Look!"

In a small street between a couple of low buildings, there was the unmistakable glint of gold. Sam rushed over and came across a golden shield. About the size of a large pizza, he wiped the dirt and moss from the front to reveal patterns set into it with jade.

"This is cool . . ." Sam said. "This looks like the zodiac. See the symbols?"

"Look here too," Rapha said. Before him were piles of gold, from carved idols to disks and coins and swords, packed into rotted-out wooden barrels. "Looks like they were all stacked up here to take out in a hurry."

"But they didn't get away—if this was the Spanish or Portuguese, they'd not leave this treasure behind."

Rapha nodded.

"We need to search for the Gear," Sam said, pulling his mind into focus. "Any of this feel familiar, from your dream?"

"It is a very strange thing . . . like I've seen it before," Rapha puzzled.

Sam chuckled.

"What?"

"It's just that's exactly what it feels like," Sam said, sorting through more and more gold objects and carvings.

"Déjà vu. We all feel it sometimes, that we're experiencing something familiar, that we've done before. As Dreamers, we dream it and then we live it. And this is all gold here—no Gear."

"We need to get to higher ground," Rapha said, distracted, pointing away from them. "Up there."

"Let's check it out."

From where they stood they could see across the old tree trunks to a stone roof, covering an altar. There was a helmet resting on it. They left the gold and made their way towards the altar, climbing more steep stone stairs on their hands and knees. The stone floor around the altar was covered with knee-high grass. They walked through it.

"This is Portuguese," Rapha said, picking up the helmet.

"And here's an armored vest," Sam said, pulling it out of the grass. "And another, and another."

All around them there were maybe twenty sets of armor.

"They made a stand here," Sam said. "Protecting something."

"Or someone . . ." Rapha said. "The expedition leader?"

Sam stood next to Rapha, who was looking down at a spot he'd cleared. There was a set of vest armor that was intricate and ornate—not one worn by a humble foot soldier.

"It's here," Rapha said, rummaging around under the armor. "I can . . . feel it."

Sam moved through the thick tall grass to help him.

Rapha stood up. "No, I mean I can *really* feel it."

Sam saw that Rapha had something in his hands. Sam came to stand next to him, peering at it closely, the dull gray sky above them not making the identification easy. In Rapha's hands, covered in a fine layer of silt, was a round object made up of several cogs. He wiped his thumb over the face of the largest gear, removing the patina of filth.

"This is it, isn't it?" Rapha said.

Sam rubbed more, cleaning it off all around until—

"Yes!" Sam said. "We've got it!"

"Who's *we*, Sam?" a voice boomed.

Sam turned around.

Hans!

And about ten armed men, all of them traitorous German Guardians, all with weapons pointing at Sam and Rapha. Now it was Sam and Rapha who were trapped on top of the altar platform, just as five centuries ago the Portuguese soldiers had been.

"I take it they're not our friends," Rapha said out the side of his mouth.

"You guessed about right," Sam said, weighing up his options.

"Two choices . . ." Hans called out to them. "Run and your friend here dies, and I then take that Gear from your unconscious body. Or hand it over, and he gets to live."

EVA

The cops had gone downstairs, pulling Mac's office apart for any clue where to find him. Eva stood with Lora and the Russian Guardian in the office above.

"The guy who posed as Mac isn't talking," Lora said. "At least, he's not saying anything of any use—he's just a paid actor from the local improv group. He had no idea that it was a legit police operation. He thought I was an actor too and that this was some sort of audition he was taking part in."

"Great," Eva said. "So what do we do now?"

Lora's phone rang, and she answered it on speaker-phone.

"We made an appointment to see each other," Mac's voice drawled out. "I can see *you*. But can you see me?"

Lora spun around, Eva too, and the four Guardians began checking the room.

"Oh really? I don't think I'm there," Mac said. "Not in the building, no. But look outside, to the lake. You'll see a strobing light."

They all looked through the glass and sure enough,

a tiny speck of a boat was strobing a powerful beacon at them.

"You see," Mac said, "I knew that you wouldn't play fair. I knew that you'd bring the authorities with you. But you see, I can't have that. You have to give me the chance to tell you what really happened."

"Did you attack the Council?" Lora asked.

"No, of course not. Why would I? But I knew no one would believe me, after leaving the Council in the way that I did. I was justifiably concerned that people might jump to conclusions. Everyone seems to be losing their heads over this race."

"But what about the whereabouts of the missing Councillors?"

"I have no idea about that."

"But what about Sam and Zara?" Lora insisted. "What about what you did to them in France?"

"A simple disagreement about how best to proceed," Mac said smoothly. "But I'd really prefer to have this meeting in more comfortable surroundings."

"What are you suggesting?" Lora asked.

"If you want to talk, to hear my side of it—to learn what you need to win this race, then come to my little boat. Bring your Dreamer friend too, since I know she's listening in. I have a proposal for you. It concerns Sam—in fact, all the Dreamers and the Gears that they seek. But just you and your friend—no one else. You have my word that once we talk, you can go. But hear me out, because I think it best that we be wise."

"Wise?" Lora asked.

"You know my connections, my power," Mac said. "I can get this done, against all the others. Hear me out."

Lora looked to Eva, her expression asking—*shall we go?*

Eva nodded.

I've come this far to help in the race, now it's my chance to really make a difference.

The Russian Guardian, close-by, grunted, "Mac, you harm them, and I'll tear your puny little boat apart with my bare hands."

Eva nearly chuckled—she liked this Guardian.

"Ah, Guardians . . ." Mac said. "I do wonder why it is that those charged with keeping the peace are always so keen to destroy things."

The Guardian looked at Lora and shook his head. It was clear he didn't like this new plan at all.

"OK," Lora said. "We'll be there soon."

34

SAM

Sam and Rapha had no choice but to surrender. Three of the men tied up Sam and Rapha and then stood guard over them with their guns. Sam grimly named them Dopey, Grumpy and Happy in his mind.

"What do we do?" asked Rapha, seated next to Sam on the ground, ankles tied out in front of them, their hands tied behind their backs.

"We get out of here," Sam said. "*And* we get that Gear."

"You two, shut it," Grumpy said to them, then moved off to sift through a pile of gold.

"Man," Rapha said, struggling with his bonds that were tied tight. "Soon as I get out of these . . ."

"What, you going to beat us up?" Dopey said, then walked off to join his mate in wonder at the great wealth scattered across the valley floor.

Sam watched as Hans cleaned the Gear with water from his canteen, chuckling at his victory. He walked down to join his other men in surveying the treasure before them.

"Say, Rapha," Sam said, loud enough for Happy to hear. "All this gold, whaddya reckon it's worth?"

"Worth? It's priceless," Rapha said. "A hoard like this, telling an amazing chapter in an unknown period of this people's lives—"

"Seriously? You ever thought of a career as a tour guide?" Sam whispered at Rapha meaningfully. "I mean," Sam said loudly, trying to make his friend understand what he was doing, "how *much* do you think it's worth?"

"Oh, right . . ." Rapha said. "Well, of course, a lot of the pieces could easily sell on the black market to collectors for millions of dollars. *Each.* All those piles of smaller trinkets, some of the ingots I saw over there, putting a weight value on it at today's prices . . . I reckon there's a couple of billion dollars' worth of gold there, easy."

"Yeah, that's what I thought," Sam said, nonchalant, and he watched with a fire in his eyes as Happy walked over to a stack of gold bars and lost himself in the possibilities at his fingertips. "A couple of billion dollars . . ."

"Sam," Rapha said out the corner of his mouth. "What are you doing?"

"Improvising . . ." Sam said, wriggling around to a new position where he spied a sharp edge he could lean his wrist ropes against. "Let's get outta here."

Sam struggled against his ropes—then stopped cold when he spied something unusual under him. What he thought were lumps and rocks in the mossy ground cover were actually *skeletons.*

"I think we've found the bodies that belonged to that

armor," Rapha said.

There were over a dozen skeletons, laid out in a haphazard semicircle with their backs to the wall as Sam and Rapha now sat.

"This is where they made their final stand," Rapha said. "And the locals later took all their armor and put it on top of the altar as an offering to the gods. Or a sign to others from the outside world."

The skull nearest Sam, still with a conquistador helmet of the age, had an arrow stuck through the eye socket. Then Sam saw something else—something very useful.

"Well, it's not going to be *our* last stand," Sam said, picking a short sword from the body, and using its edge to cut through his ropes and then Rapha's. They scrambled over to the low wall where they saw Hans' men loading packs with gold.

"There," Sam said, pointing to the Gear sitting on top of one of the packs. It was between them and the rest of the men. "But where's Hans?"

"Right here . . ."

Sam turned to face the voice, to see Hans smiling down at him, his pistol in his hand.

"Going somewhere, boys?"

"No," Sam said calmly. "But you are."

Before Hans could react, Sam lashed out with a leg flip that put Hans on his back—and he knocked his head on a conquistador's helmet as he landed. There was a hollow thud and he was out cold.

"Come on, that's our cue to exit the scene," Sam said and scurried close to the ground to get what they had come for. He slipped the Gear into his retrieved backpack, all the while watching as Hans' men continued to scoop all the gold they could carry into their packs, oblivious that their commander was down and out. Rapha tapped Sam on the shoulder, pointing to the low building that they'd entered from and started creeping towards it.

"Hey!" a German voice rang out. "Stop!"

"Run for it!" Sam yelled as they sprinted across the hidden valley of gold.

ALEX

"Tell me again how you talked me into this?" Shiva asked, getting his avatar ready behind the wheel of a beat-up taxi.

"Because," Alex replied, climbing the seemingly never-ending ladder of the crane, "you said that Matrix will recognize your game play. So you start messing with him and getting his attention and then you race back this way . . ."

"He'll follow me, yeah, I know the plan," Shiva said. "But I think you'll find that he'll vaporize me as soon as he sees me."

"You said you had mad gaming skills."

"Um, yeah," Shiva said, revving his engine. "OK, well, I guess it's now or never. You ready up there?"

"Almost at the controls, so yeah, go for it in three secs."

"If you hear an angry scream and a big explosion, don't worry, it's just that I've been vaporized."

"Go!" Alex insisted.

"OK, OK . . . pushy."

Alex reached the top of the crane as he heard Shiva

burning rubber, flooring the taxi.

"I'm in the crane control room!" Alex said.

"He's seen me!" Shiva yelled.

The gunfire from the tank started up, rounds from the smaller turrets blasting away at the road all around Shiva while still peppering the other hundred or so players making futile attempts to take down the armored beast.

Alex knew he'd only have one chance at this, if he was to have any hope of beating Matrix in that mechanical monster of a tank.

"He's chasing me back towards you!" Shiva yelled. "He knows it's me in here!"

"Good!" Alex was inside the control room of the crane, and he started to pull levers and flick switches to see what was controlling what.

"Ten seconds—he's fast!" Shiva said, and Alex could see that his friend, way down below in a tiny little taxi, was being hotly pursued by Matrix. Lines of machine gun fire tore up the ground behind the taxi. It was obvious Matrix was enjoying the chase and wanted to run his former colleague off the edge of the pier and into the water.

"That's it!" Alex called. "Keep at it!"

BOOM!

The huge main cannon fired and the shell hit the end of the pier, turning it into a pile of broken concrete and twisted metal.

"Five seconds!" Alex called, measuring the time between the tank and his crane.

"He's right on my tail," Shiva said.

"Three!"

"He's going to run me over!" Shiva said, and it looked that way as the taxi flashed underneath the crane and then the tank rumbled through.

Alex brought the huge hook up, right at the moment the turret's barrel was underneath, throwing a lever and lifting—just enough, before the massive steel cables snapped tight, disrupting the forward momentum of the tank.

It happened in slow motion. The snared barrel caused the war machine to twist on one side. It lifted off at a back corner and continued to twist and roll, until it seemed to hang precariously on one edge of its track—

And stayed there for five full seconds until its weight shifted, just enough.

The tank slipped off the side of the pier with an almighty splash of water that swept over everything in sight.

"Yeeeeee-ha!" Alex called. "We got him! He's out of commission!"

Alex climbed from the control booth and saw dozens of friendly fighters moving towards the sinking tank, tossing charges all over it to blow it to bits.

"Shiva?" Alex looked around. "Buddy, you there? Shiva? Shiva?"

His heart sank and he realized his friend must have died in the game when—

Alex saw the beat-up taxi rattle to a stop down below.

"That's my name!" Shiva called out. "Don't wear it out, Thor—god of war games!"

"Yeah!" Alex said, pulling off his headgear to give Shiva a high five back in the real world. "We did it! Take *that*, Matrix!"

36

EVA

Eva sat in the chair next to Lora, who powered the tiny speedboat out to the much larger cruiser on Lake Michigan.

"You sure about this?" Eva asked, looking back to see if she could spot the helicopter full of Guardians that was lurking somewhere over the city, ready to rush in and storm Mac's boat.

"No. But we don't have much choice—we need to hear Mac out, figure out his motives and see if he can be reasoned with."

"Why?"

"Sam is the reason we came here in the first place."

"Because we have enough enemies?"

"That's right," Lora said. "And Mac is very well connected, very powerful—he is influential, especially among the American military. Whether we like him or not, it would be a real blow to lose his support." Lora eased off the throttle and guided the little boat up against the luxury yacht, catching a line tossed down to them. "You have to pick your battles, Eva. The trick is to know when to be diplomatic and when to be tough."

"And which time is this?" Eva asked.

"We're about to find out."

I'm not sure I like the sound of that.

Inside Mac's huge luxury yacht, Eva sat in the lounge next to Lora. Mac sat opposite, relaxing in a large chair. There were no security guys visible, just an elegant maid who served them supper.

"It seems, from what you've said," Mac said to Lora, "that you want me to join you—join the Academy and Council's quest in this race."

"That would be our hope," Lora said.

"Well, now hear my offer," Mac said.

"Your offer?" Eva said. "Lora's barely finished speaking, and what, you're just chucking that back in her face?"

Mac smiled at Eva and said, "You're a smart one, Eva. Good. You'll need to be." He stood and paced around the floor. "You see, I agree with you, Lora, on one point—we *should* work together. But I'm not in agreement that the Academy should be involved."

"Lora works there," Eva said. "You know that."

Mac continued undeterred. "What I am offering is the full might of the US military machine. Think about it. We can use them to stop Hans and Stella dead in their tracks.

The Enterprise and the Academy too. You work with me, you're on the winning team."

He stopped and gave Lora a long hard stare.

"In exchange for what?" she asked. "What do you want from us?"

"Isn't it obvious?" Eva said. The two looked to her. She only had eyes for Mac, and her expression was full of fury. "He wants you to deliver the Dreamers, because that's what he *doesn't* have. He wants you to be a double agent, to work for the Professor, but give him information about the last 13, where they're going, where the Gear is."

Mac nodded. "Smart girl."

"Then we're both smart," Lora said, standing. "Come on, Eva, this man has nothing to offer us."

"Oh, really?" Mac said, his tone as if he held all the cards. "You think we're done here?"

"I'm done talking," Lora said.

"And I'm done listening," Eva added.

"Hmm. As you'll see, I realized long ago that to succeed you sometimes need to make unpleasant alliances," Mac said, a crazed look now flitting into his eyes. "You can't beat *him*, Lora, you should know that. So I'm giving you a final chance to join us."

"Us?" Lora said, pulling Eva to her and pushing towards the door.

But the door flung open as they turned to it and a darkness filled the doorway.

"Yes . . ." came the deep, metallic voice. "*Us.*"

Mac's working with Solaris!

Lora stood in front of Eva, watching as Solaris and Mac both closed in on them. Eva shrank from Solaris' gaze and frantically looked for another way out. There was none.

We're trapped. Caught in Mac's trap.

"You see, I made *him* an offer, too," Mac was saying. "I had something *he* needed. So we cut a deal."

"What could you have that he would want or need?" Lora muttered.

"Access," Mac said.

"To what?" Lora said.

Mac looked at Solaris, who stood there, silent and resolute.

"Why," Mac said, "I thought that would be obvious. All the Academy and Council information, getting the two of you here. Not to mention the bomb at the Academy . . . oh, I know it didn't do its job, but not to worry. It flushed you out here, hoping for a truce. And now the Professor will do anything to get the two of you back. Am I right?"

Eva shook with fear and with anger. Lora turned to her, silently willing her to accept their fate— for now.

You have to pick your battles? We've well and truly lost this one.

37

SAM

"They're close behind us!" Rapha said.

"Yep," Sam replied, running down the stairs. "Follow me and don't hesitate!"

He jumped up on the steeply slanted stone balustrade covered in damp moss and slid down, picking up incredible speed by the time he reached the bottom and shot off the end as if from a cannon. He stumbled across the floor of the landing, Rapha not far behind him, landing in an awkward tumble.

"Come on," Sam said, helping his friend to his feet and the two of them ran down the tunnel to the right, soon coming to the booby-trapped chamber again. The stone wall was still in place, blocking their escape.

"Run and jump to the first monkey!" Sam said behind Rapha, and he didn't need to be told twice. With a long stride, Rapha made it to the first monkey, Sam landing to his left on another monkey tile.

"Now what?" Rapha said.

"The tile you stood on before that triggered the wall," Sam said, "it had a spider on it. And there *must* be a way of resetting the chamber otherwise how could they get in and out?" He looked at Rapha with a shrug. "It has to be worth a try, right?"

Sam pressed his foot gingerly on a spider engraving.

A grinding noise made them jump.

I hope I haven't just made things worse . . .

The stone wall slowly rumbled in front of them, sliding upward and back into the recessed ceiling above.

"Nice!" Rapha said. He readied himself and leapt to the next group of monkey tiles, Sam following.

They caught their breath at the landing at the top of the spiral stairs, but not before Sam went back and stepped on a spider tile.

CLONK!

Another stone wall came down from the ceiling as Sam leapt to safety.

"That should slow them up for a while," Sam said.

Rapha nodded and sucked at the air, too exhausted to talk and they set off down into the darkness. Breathless, they emerged out onto the stone ledge where they'd landed in the ultralight.

"Oh no!" Rapha cried.

"What?" Sam spun around, expecting to see one of his enemies standing there.

But there was no one.

"They've disabled the plane!" Rapha said.

"Can you fix it?" Sam asked.

"They've cut the fuel line," Rapha said, "and removed the spark plug. It's not flying anywhere."

"Well, we have to get off this ledge," Sam said. He looked around, his hope fading.

Rapha stared at his ultralight. "I have an idea," he said.

Sam watched him working, realizing within a few seconds what Rapha was thinking.

"Good thinking, do it," Sam said. "We dismount the wing then we can hang on to the crossbar underneath."

"And use it to glide down to the basin level below."

Sam kept watch, wary of Hans' men appearing. As he looked around, something by his feet seemed out of place. There were footprints in the dirt. Big, like the combat boots of . . .

Agents.

"Rapha . . ." Sam said, looking over to his friend as he unhooked the large glider wing. "How could Hans' guys get down here and attack your plane? I mean, they must have discovered another way to get to the city, not up this cliff face."

Rapha shook his head as if he was trying to make sense of it as he held the wing up above his head, then stopped and looked back at Sam with a shocked expression.

"Sam—behind you!" he called out frantically.

Sam turned. An Agent was slumped over there, ten yards away, bending over against the cliff wall. He had climbing gear on . . . he wasn't moving. Sam went over to him. He'd been shot through the neck by a skinny arrow.

"He's dead," Sam said. "A couple of them must have been here—I don't think this guy had time to mess with our plane. Looks like he stood on the wrong tile then staggered back out."

"There's no one here now," Rapha urged, turning away from the dead body. "We must jump quickly before they come back."

Sam threw the Agent's pistol into the waterfall and grabbed the radio headset. He put it on and immediately heard Stella's voice giving out commands to her troops.

"OK, we're out of the tunnel system," Stella said. "Most of them just lead to lookouts in the cliffs. Keep your wits about you, I just heard shouting."

"We have to go," Sam said quietly to Rapha, who now had the hang glider wing fully detached and held up high. He stood next to Rapha, gripping the bar overhead. "With any luck they'll take care of Hans' guys—"

A piercing scream echoed from the tunnel entrance behind them.

"That'd be someone else stepping on the wrong tile," Sam winced.

"Ready?" Rapha asked.

Sam looked out at the jungle swathed in silver clouds. He could still tell that the drop from up there was immense.

"Not really," he said. "But that's never stopped me before."

"Let's go," Rapha said. "Run as fast as you can, and when we clear the ledge, lean away from the cliff."

"Got it."

"OK."

"Wait—no countdown?" Sam asked.

"All right. One," Rapha said. "Two . . ."

"Three," they said in unison, running full pelt with the glider canopy held over their heads until the ground gave way beneath them and then they were soaring into the cloud cover below. Sam's heart jumped into his throat as he forced himself not to look down. He turned to Rapha who was grinning from ear to ear.

THUD! THUD! THUD!

The third shot he felt. A dart had hit the back of his leg, but his Stealth Suit protected him. He looked over his shoulder. There stood Stella on the ledge, dart gun in her hand.

"That was—" Sam trailed off. Next to him, Rapha was slipping into unconsciousness, two darts in his back, his grip on the bar above quickly loosening.

"Rapha!" Sam shouted, "Rapha, *hang on!*"

Rapha passed out, letting go of the bar and tipping backward away from Sam. Sam threw out his arm and caught Rapha's left wrist. "Wake up, Rapha!" he yelled but he knew it was no use.

As they spun helplessly out of control in the air, he heard Stella's laugh echo around them.

"Try getting out of this one, Sam!" her voice sneered from high above.

Rapha dangled from Sam's grip, getting heavier by the moment, pulling them downward and towards the rocks of the jagged mountainside. His jacket started to come loose—

RIP!

Sam watched in horror as the tear widened, pulling Rapha further away from his slipping grip.

No, I can't lose him.

Sam's arm burned as he frantically tried to hold on to Rapha. He closed his eyes as the cliff face came crashing towards them.